Vignettes & Verses

Udayan Banerjee and Metali Banerjee

Published by Udayan Banerjee, 2024.

VIGNETTES & VERSES

First edition. April 24, 2024.

Copyright © 2024 Udayan Banerjee and Metali Banerjee.

ISBN: 979-8224396214

Written by Udayan Banerjee and Metali Banerjee.

VIGNETTES & VERSES

Whispers of Life, Woven in Words

Metali Banerjee
Udayan Banerjee

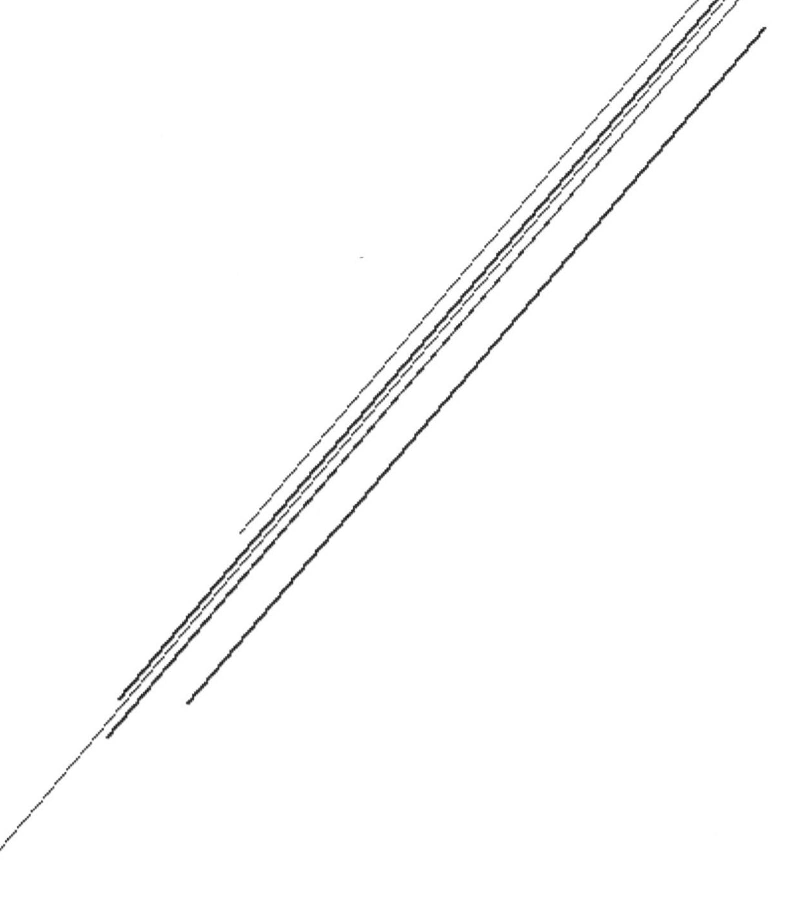

Copyright

First edition: October 2023
Edited by: Udayan Banerjee
Cover art by: Udayan Banerjee

Foreword

The book "Vignettes and Verses" chronicles the remarkable journey of a couple who, undeterred by numerous obstacles, chose to face life's challenges hand in hand. I extend my heartfelt appreciation to Udayan (my brother) and Metali (sister-in-law) for bringing forth this literary gem. It offers a vivid glimpse into their days filled with joy, as well as their trials, tribulations, and the tenacity with which they confronted every situation.

Metali's extraordinary journey, marked by the profound responsibility of raising her siblings following the untimely demise of her parents when she was just seventeen, stands as both a testament to her resilience and an inspiration to us all.

Udayan was a man of conscience, harbouring dreams of entrepreneurship. Along his journey, he encountered numerous peaks and valleys, emerging even stronger in the face of adversity. The chapter delving into their shared passion for travel and audacious aspirations is particularly captivating. It beautifully emphasizes that it is through dreaming that one truly achieves greatness.

In the concluding chapter, we are guided down a path of moral rectitude and spiritual enlightenment, steeped in the practices of Buddhism. Their unwavering faith in this philosophy saw them through many a severe trial.

In summation, I wholeheartedly recommend 'Vignettes and Verses' to all. The authors' eloquent prose is not only a source of motivation but also an inspiration, weaving a tapestry of beauty and wisdom.

Dr. Quaylee Chakraborty
Educationist

Preface

Our Journey of Trials, Triumphs, and Enduring Love

In July of 1981, we embarked on a journey together, bound by the sacred bond of marriage. Since then, our path has been filled with a tapestry of experiences – from the heart-wrenching and perilous birth of our second child to moments of hardship that seemed never-ending. We took upon ourselves the responsibility of raising Mita's younger brother and sister, a promise we made to each other to uphold till the end of our days. However, life threw us a curveball when Mita's brother, Babla, vanished for three years, grappling with the challenges of both employment and schizophrenia in Ludhiana.

It's safe to say that there hasn't been a single moment of respite in our journey. We faced each day with unyielding determination, weathering the storms that life sent our way. We further complicated matters by leaving a promising position at Maruti, and venturing into our own business, only to face failure in the end. We managed to claw our way back, thanks to a resurgence of effort just before retirement. Only we, and the Higher Power above, truly understood the depths of our struggles.

As our business gained traction, so did our hopes for a life free from want. Mita was urged to step down from her role as an educator at the esteemed DPS school, with promises of a more relaxed existence on the horizon. We even treated ourselves to a two-week sojourn in Europe, a testament to our newfound optimism. Little did I realize that lurking behind the façade of progress were unforeseen challenges.

Our business faltered, thrusting us into a sea of financial uncertainty. We became sizable debtors, teetering on the brink of a precipice. Udayan, with ingenuity, managed to secure technical consultancy work, while Mita secured a position with the esteemed Times of India to stave off impending financial disaster. The daily commute, particularly for Mita, was gruelling, involving commuting by bus with three changes to reach her office, though she was used to a chauffeur-driven car. Udayan, on the other hand, transformed his car into an impromptu office, battling the sweltering Gurgaon summer without the luxury of air conditioning. We were unable to afford even the rent for our accommodation when a kind friend extended the offer of an unfurnished dwelling, without asking for rent. We navigated through this tumultuous period, narrowly escaping the precipice.

Fortuitously, our heavily invested factory was acquired, under the stipulation that Udayan would continue to oversee its operations. However, we received no financial reprieve, as our net worth had plummeted to zero under the weight of mounting debts.

Now, we stand at the threshold of retirement, our bodies carrying the weight of various health concerns. Udayan approaches seventy, while Mita is sixty-two. Our financial burdens now rest on the shoulders of our sons. A flat we acquired towards the end of Udayan's career has proven to be a providential asset, sparing us the expense of rent in our twilight years.

'Vignettes and Verses' encapsulates the expressions of our hearts and minds, woven over the years. Some may perceive these writings as boastful, but those who truly understand will discern the profound struggles that have fueled these verses.

May you find solace and inspiration in these pages.

Metali Banerjee

Udayan Banerjee

1

Navigating the Symphony of Aches and Memories

Harmonising Life's Melodies, One Memory at a Time

As the first rays of dawn gently brush the horizon, I rise from my slumber, a symphony of aches and pains accompanying me. The calendar pages are flipping towards seventy, adorned with the weight of co-morbidities. It's a stark contrast to the days of yore, when each morning was a joyful overture, leaving yesterday behind. In my youth, pain had a different face - a cricket ball meeting my lips, parting them with an exuberant force, or a hockey ball striking my shin, a cry of pain echoing through the fields. Yet, at the dawn of those days, there were no aches, no twinges, just the promise of a new day.

Today, the quail's mellifluous song serenades the morning, joined in chorus by fellow avians, heralding the sun's advent. Meanwhile, an orchestra of discomfort plays within my limbs and spinal cord, its notes etched in silence. I bear it stoically, unable to voice the quiet symphony of my inner world.

The reminiscence takes me back to a time when the pain was ephemeral, a companion swiftly ushered away by the balm of medical care. Oh, how I yearned for those days when the promise of recovery meant a swift return to the cricket pitch.

I recall a particular practice session, donning the gloves as the keeper. A renowned fast bowler stood poised, and with resolve, I decided to stand up to his fiery deliveries. Back then, the mat on the 22-yard pitch ensured the ball's formidable bounce. I held my ground, pocketing several deliveries, until one descended like a meteor between me and the sun. A resounding impact - the ball met my lips with unyielding force, reopening an old wound. Blood flowed, and momentarily, I surrendered to darkness. With the help of teammates, I found shelter beneath the shade of a wise old tree. Clutching a handkerchief to my upper lip, I pedalled six kilometres to a defence nursing station. There, stitches mended my lips, painkillers provided solace, and after three days, I was back on the field, cricket bat in hand.

Today, I traverse the hours, a silent companion of pain. Despite my disposition towards optimism, I cannot help but wince at the intensity of my struggle, a silent symphony conducted within.

-Udayan

2

My First Born: A Journey of Love, Sacrifice and Growth

From Birth to Blooming; A Parent's Precious Odyssey

This narrative encompasses the story of my eldest child, not necessarily presented in chronological order.

The summer of 1981 marked a turning point in my life, a pivotal moment that set the stage for a story of love, sacrifice, and growth. It was a season of beginnings, as I embarked on my first job in the vibrant city of Hyderabad, India. Meanwhile, in the city of Kanpur, a young woman named Mita, who would later become my wife, was facing immense challenges in her own life.

Mita's journey had been anything but easy. At the tender age of fourteen, she had to bid farewell to her mother, leaving behind an ailing father and two younger siblings, a brother and a sister, both barely in their young years. Tragedy struck once again when her father passed away just three years later. With her siblings still in school and entirely dependent on her, Mita shouldered the immense responsibility of being a parent figure. Balancing her education and the demands of a full-time job at a bank, she worked tirelessly to make ends meet.

From my vantage point in Hyderabad, I witnessed Mita's struggles with a heavy heart. The miles between us seemed to stretch farther, creating an emotional divide that yearned to be bridged. Mita's days were a blur of activity—early mornings preparing breakfast for her siblings, followed by classes for her graduate program, and then off to the bank. Often, she'd work late, returning home to guide her brother and sister through their studies before finally tending to her own. Her relentless routine took its toll, and the thought of her enduring such hardship alone weighed heavily on my soul.

Amid these trying times, a moment of clarity dawned on me one night. I awoke, my head resting on my father's lap in the Air Force

Academy in Dundigal, Hyderabad, where he was stationed before his retirement. My father's wisdom and support were the bedrock that held me steady. I confided my worries about Mita's plight, and his advice became the beacon that guided our path. He suggested that I marry Mita and bring her, along with her brother and sister, to Hyderabad. It was a simple yet profound solution. But concerns about the financial strain gnawed at me, with my father's impending retirement and the need to support my younger brother's education. In his characteristic wisdom, my father assured me that he would handle my brother's education from his pension post-retirement. He encouraged me to take the plunge, to marry Mita and create a new life for her family in Hyderabad.

Mita, at the time, was employed at Standard Chartered Bank, and its branches were not present in Hyderabad. I asked her to resign and embrace my father's plan, even though it meant disappointment for her.

With Mita's wholehearted agreement, less than a month later, we stood before the sacred fire, united in marriage on July 10, 1981. I carefully packed her belongings, sent them to our new home in Hyderabad, and welcomed her brother and sister into our lives. It was a demanding period, but we weathered through. Mita's sister was enrolled in a reputable school, continuing her education, while her brother embarked on a Science program at Osmania University.

Our life slowly found its rhythm, yet Mita couldn't erase the scars of her early losses. It was during this time that we decided to expand our family, believing that the arrival of a child would bring healing and joy.

And so, we welcomed our first child into the world. My father bestowed upon him the name Abhishek, signifying a 'coronation', convinced that this child would illuminate the fortunes of our departed family. As the days turned into months, we transitioned to an apartment nearer to my workplace, bidding farewell to the comfort of my father's residence. I secured a position with the new Maruti project in Gurgaon, prompting our move when Abhishek was just three months old. On a chilly January morning, we arrived in Delhi, preparing for the final leg of our journey to the then small village of Gurgaon.

My work was demanding, often consuming long hours, leaving me with scarce moments to spend with our son. Nonetheless, the joy of fatherhood was immeasurable, and I treasured every fleeting second with him. Affectionately known as Appu, he brought boundless happiness into our lives.

As Appu blossomed, we observed the seeds of his kind and orderly nature take root. From a young age, he displayed an inclination towards cleanliness, picking up litter, even if it wasn't his own, and disposing of it thoughtfully. This sense of orderliness spread to those around him, including us adults, teaching us a valuable lesson in keeping our surroundings clean.

Appu's spirit of sharing extended beyond objects; he generously gave away his toys and books to less fortunate children, imparting this lesson of compassion to his younger brother, Abhi. This innate kindness and generosity remained with both of them as they ventured into adolescence.

At the tender age of ten, Appu displayed a remarkable level of compassion and selflessness that belied his years. It was on his birthday, a day usually reserved for joyous celebrations with friends, that he approached his mother with an earnest plea. Instead of marking the occasion with festivities, he implored her to allocate the funds towards a different cause - the purchase of books, notebooks, and pencils for those less fortunate.

His request was born out of a genuine concern for the welfare of others, particularly those who lacked access to even the most basic educational resources. In a world where most children his age were engrossed in their own desires and whims, Appu's heart was inclined towards a higher purpose, one that aimed to uplift those in need.

With his mother's wholehearted support, they embarked on a mission to make a tangible difference in the lives of the underprivileged. Together, they carefully selected an assortment of essential learning materials, each one representing a small step towards a brighter future for the children who would receive them.

The destination of their benevolent endeavour was a nearby slum, a place where hardship and adversity were all too familiar. Appu, armed with a sense of purpose and determination, ventured into this community, ready to make a positive impact. As he distributed the books, notebooks, and pencils, a wave of gratitude and hope washed over the faces of the children who received them.

At that moment, Appu's gesture went far beyond the material objects he offered. He provided a glimmer of opportunity, a chance for these young minds to cultivate knowledge and envision a world beyond their current circumstances. It was a small act of kindness that had the potential to sow the seeds of transformation, not just for the individuals involved, but for the community as a whole.

This selfless act became a testament to the depth of Appu's empathy and his unwavering commitment to making a positive impact in the world. It was a poignant reminder that even the youngest among us possess the power to effect change, uplift others, and inspire a spirit of generosity and kindness that can ripple through society.

As the years passed, Appu's compassionate nature continued to shape his character, leaving an indelible mark on those fortunate enough to know him. His story serves as a beacon of hope and a powerful reminder that acts of kindness, no matter how small, have the potential to create a brighter, more inclusive world for us all.

The memories of Appu's childhood have left an indelible mark on our hearts, like cherished pages in the book of our family history. Among the myriad of recollections, one particular incident stands out vividly in my mind.

I remember a time when Appu's desire for a packet of Maggi noodles was so intense that it seemed to devour his thoughts. So one steamy afternoon in the summer, he climbed down the stairs of our first-floor flat and lumbered away to a shop nearby to buy his favourite Maggi noodles. However, he found himself in a predicament, lacking the funds to satisfy this craving. It was during this moment of yearning that our trusted household maid, perhaps sensing his eagerness, intervened with a heartwarming gesture. She promised to procure the coveted noodles for him herself, turning Appu's longing into a moment of joy and anticipation.

This simple incident, while seemingly insignificant, became a hallmark of Appu's formative years. It symbolized not only his fondness for a particular snack but also the purity of childhood desires and the innocence of moments that create lasting memories. It was a glimpse into the charm of those early years when the world was painted in vibrant hues of wonder and excitement, and every small pleasure held immeasurable significance.

As time flowed on, the memory of this incident remained a cherished part of our family lore, a testament to the precious and sometimes whimsical nature of childhood. It served as a reminder of the simple joys that unite us and, even in their seemingly trivial form, become the threads that weave the rich tapestry of our shared experiences.

On a separate occasion, at the tender age of six, Appu made a decision that left me both astounded and deeply moved. It was the eve of Diwali, the cherished festival of lights, a time when homes are aglow with lamps and hearts are filled with joy. Yet, Appu, in his youthful wisdom, chose to abstain from the festivities. His reason, however, was far beyond his years.

He displayed an uncanny understanding of the plight of children who toiled tirelessly in the hazardous trade of crafting firecrackers, an industry that marred the purity of the festival. It was as though Appu had tapped into a source of wisdom beyond his years, a perspective that transcended the ordinary.

In the face of our plans to join a friend's Diwali celebration, Appu's resolute stance held a profound message. He advocated for a celebration that did not come at the cost of another's well-being, a sentiment that resonated deeply within our family.

This remarkable display of empathy and moral conviction illuminated Appu's character, leaving an indelible mark on all who were fortunate enough to witness it. It was a moment that spoke volumes about his innate sense of justice and compassion, traits that would go on to define his journey in life.

As we reflect on that emotional Diwali night, Appu's actions serve as a poignant reminder that wisdom often transcends age and that even the youngest among us can be beacons of light, guiding us towards a path of greater understanding, compassion, and social responsibility.

From his early years, Appu possessed a striking resemblance to a Bollywood child prodigy. His cherubic features and endearing charm were impossible to ignore. What further enriched his journey was the fortuitous blessing of being surrounded by teachers who showered him with love and provided invaluable guidance at every juncture, from his initial foray into school to his later years in college. This nurturing environment became the cornerstone of his academic and personal growth, sculpting him into the fine individual he would eventually become. Each institution he attended became a fertile ground for his development, thanks to the dedicated educators who recognised and nurtured his potential. Their influence would continue to resonate throughout his life, leaving an indelible mark on his path to maturity and success.

Family excursions, particularly to the nearby Himalayan mountains, held a special place in our hearts. I'd fold down the back seat of my trusty Maruti, creating a snug space for the boys, and off we'd go on our adventures. These trips were steeped in joy, laughter, and the uncomplicated pleasures of life.

As Appu matured into a tall and self-assured young man, new challenges and opportunities awaited him. His academic prowess shone through, culminating in a degree in History, even though his heart was drawn to the world of finance. He followed his instincts, pursuing a management program that further honed his skills and prepared him for the corporate arena.

Another significant chapter unfolded when Appu secured his first job in Mumbai. Love blossomed between him and Bharti, his college companion, and soon, they exchanged vows. Bharti, a delightful addition to our family, became my cherished daughter-in-law.

Their journey in Mumbai was not without its hurdles, but they embraced the rhythm of the bustling city. Soon, Bharti was expecting, and my grandson, Aarush, made his grand entrance into the world. Cradling Aarush in my arms, I couldn't help but reflect on the day I held his father, Appu, in the same embrace.

Presently, Appu stands as a dedicated husband and a loving father, exemplifying the very principles of compassion, tidiness, and open-handedness that he assimilated in his formative years. His unwavering commitment to the welfare of others persists, much as it did when he was a young lad, wholeheartedly distributing his playthings and literary treasures.

The narrative that took root in the winter of 1981 has blossomed into a rich tapestry woven with threads of affection, tenacity and everlasting ties that bind our family together. It is a testament to the enduring power of love and the strength it imparts to our lives.

With a discerning eye honed over the years, Appu now employs his own well-refined judgement in bringing up his son, Aarush. This journey of parenthood is guided not only by the values instilled in him during his own upbringing but by also the wisdom and insights he has gained through his own experiences. In this way, he carries forth the legacy of nurturing and shaping the next generation, ensuring that the torch of compassion and generosity continues to burn brightly in our family's lineage.

- Udayan

3

World Peace

Walking in this era of eternal peace,
Walk hand in hand;
Reach out to the mighty river of people,
Working for their good,
With sincerity of deeds,
Purity in heart;
Work, focus on World Peace.
Hey, friends of courage and wisdom!
With your tranquil spirit,
Indomitable courage and love;
With the warmth of sunshine,
Victory in your heart;
Let this love of yours
Spread World Peace till eternity.

-Metali

4

My Second Born – A Journey of Challenges and Triumphs

Navigating Parenthood's Rollercoaster with My Second Born

Life had reached its zenith after the birth of my firstborn, Appu. We had relocated to Gurgaon due to my new job at the Maruti factory, and we settled in a housing sector. However, the town was far from developed, lacking entertainment options, and even medical facilities were scarce. The transport system between Gurgaon and Delhi left much to be desired, making every trip to the city a significant endeavour. Amid these challenging circumstances, we raised Appu.

My work at the factory was both time-consuming and physically demanding. It often required long hours and left me exhausted. To ensure Appu received the care and attention he needed, my wife, Mita, decided to enrol herself as a teacher at a local school. This allowed her to create an atmosphere of education at home, ensuring that Appu received the best possible upbringing.

As Appu grew, it became clear that he was an intelligent and affectionate child. However, due to the nature of my work and the security concerns at the factory, he was deprived of many childhood friendships. Threats of kidnapping due to labour disputes meant that he couldn't freely interact with other children or play in the nearby park. This was a challenging time for us, and Appu's yearning for companionship his age led to mood swings and frustration.

Living in a first-floor flat, we had a neighbour on the ground floor who had a daughter named Neha, who was nearly the same age as Appu. They played together occasionally, which brought some joy to Appu's life. However, our circumstances changed, and we had to move a few kilometres away to a new accommodation. This move left Appu without a playmate, and his desire for companionship weighed heavily on us as parents.

Determined not to let him grow up longing for something we couldn't provide, we made a life-altering decision – we decided to have another child so that Appu could have a sibling to play with. Appu also desired to have one baby brother or sister and he told his mother as much. Mita became pregnant, and her visits to the gynaecologist became regular. However, fate had other plans for us.

Mita was admitted to the hospital as her placenta had lowered, posing a significant risk to the baby she was carrying. Multiple stitches were performed to prevent further complications, and she was discharged with hopes of a safe pregnancy. However, a week later, she began to bleed profusely, leading to an emergency surgery. This was the moment when Abhi, our second-born, entered the world.

Born prematurely at just six and a half months, Abhi was a tiny and fragile creature. I caught a glimpse of him as he was being brought out of the operating room – his fingers resembled wax matchsticks, but his head was remarkably large and covered with a cascade of hair. It was a surreal and heart-wrenching sight. Mita, meanwhile, was stitched up and moved to a hospital room.

Access to the room where prematurely born babies were kept in incubators was restricted. I could only watch Abhi through a glass window meant for visitors like me. It was a daunting and nerve-wracking experience to witness. Numerous needles were inserted into his delicate feet and arms, and he was fed with his mother's milk, which had to be artificially squeezed out of Mita's breasts and fed to him. This routine continued for a week before he was moved to the room and kept snugly wrapped in blankets in a cradle.

Appu's excitement when Abhi finally came home was palpable. His eyes sparkled with joy as he gazed upon his baby brother, eager to hold and cuddle him. Sadly, due to Abhi's premature birth, Appu had to exercise caution, but his love and anticipation were unmistakable. At this point, Appu was six years old, and his impatience to bond with his sibling even led him to skip meals.

However, amidst this joyful period, a sombre incident occurred. My father passed away in Calcutta, and it was during this challenging time that we discovered Abhi's battle with epilepsy. Following a thorough medical examination, it was determined that this was just the beginning of the condition, and with proper treatment, he could overcome it.

Abhi's journey was a testament to the power of care and dedication. From the moment Mita took charge of his treatment, she demonstrated an unwavering commitment to his well-being. The precision with which she administered his medicines was nothing short of remarkable; it was almost as if one could set their watches by the cadence of her ministrations.

Under the watchful eye of Abhi's neonatologist, there loomed a sombre concern – the apprehension that Abhi might traverse the path of a slow learner, a prospect that cast a shadow of uncertainty over his future. It was as though a cloud hung over the potential he held within.

However, Mita was determined to defy this prognosis. She dedicated herself tirelessly, leaving no stone unturned in her pursuit of Abhi's betterment. His love and care became the scaffolding that supported Abhi's journey to recovery. Her belief in his potential was unyielding.

In the span of a mere four years, the transformation that Abhi underwent was nothing short of extraordinary. Against all odds, he not only emerged from the clutches of his initial struggles, but he soared to the pinnacle of his academic pursuits, claiming the coveted first position in his class. It was a triumph that resonated not only in his academic achievements but also in the indomitable spirit that he had acquired along the way.

Mita's unrelenting dedication, coupled with Abhi's unwavering determination, shattered the barriers that once seemed insurmountable. Their story stands as a beacon of hope, a testament to the boundless potential that lies within every individual, waiting to be nurtured and unleashed. Abhi's remarkable journey serves as a reminder that with the right support and unwavering belief, one can overcome even the most daunting challenges to emerge victorious.

Sibling relationships are often characterized by their genuineness. Growing up in the same environment, alongside parents and other family members, siblings share unique experiences and memories that foster a deep bond between them. This bond, once formed, tends to endure throughout their lives. Appu and Abhi's relationship is a testament to this enduring connection, which remains steadfast even after three decades.

For sisters, having an elder or younger brother can be a wonderful experience. Abhi, though male, however, clung to his brother like a loyal companion from a very young age. An elder brother should ideally be a friend, guide, and protector, shielding his younger sibling from the challenges of the world. Appu fulfilled this role admirably, a role he continues to play even today though Abhi resides and works in a foreign land.

Witnessing Appu's love and protective instincts towards his "Bhai" was a truly heartwarming experience. There was an innate sense of care in the way he enveloped Abhi as if creating an invisible shield against the adversities of the world.

As time passed, their bond deepened, evolving into an unbreakable connection. They shared countless moments of joy, their laughter echoing through our home. One notable feature of our residence was the expansive, roofed verandah that held an empty cot. It became the canvas for Appu's imaginative endeavours. Using Mita's old sarees, he meticulously fashioned makeshift houses for them both, creating a world of their own.

In this enchanting haven, the two brothers would immerse themselves for hours on end. Their imaginations ran wild, constructing stories and adventures within the walls of their make-believe homes. It was a sanctuary of play, a space where their young hearts thrived on the boundless possibilities that their creativity conjured. These were the cherished moments that etched themselves into the tapestry of their childhood, a testament to the enduring power of sibling love and shared imagination.

One day, while we were all sitting and chatting in the living room, we overheard Appu speaking to his brother in an unusually gentle and pleasing tone, saying, "Abhi, please don't do it." This departure from his typical manner of speech immediately caught my attention, as Appu, despite his deep affection for his brother, rarely used such sweet and gentle language. Curious, I got up from my chair and peeked into the bedroom where they were playing. What I witnessed left me laughing heartily. Appu lay sprawled bare-chested on the floor, while Abhi, who had grown plump over the years, sat atop him, enthusiastically pounding his fists on Appu's chest, akin to a scene from a Tarzan movie. In return, Appu playfully pummeled Abhi's back with both hands, all the while maintaining his sweet tone to reassure us that everything was fine between them.

As Appu continued to grow, it became apparent that he had a talent for singing, a gift that ran in our family. I was keen on nurturing this talent and enrolled him in classical music classes with a nearby instructor. Appu was in the sixth grade at the time. Interestingly, Abhi, observing his brother's music lessons, expressed a keen desire to join as well, even though he was just three years old. Although we had initially planned to enrol him in music classes at a later age, his unwavering determination led us to start his lessons immediately, including learning to play the tabla. Abhi was overjoyed to attend the classes alongside his beloved Appu, holding his hand all the way.

Then, one day, a sudden incident unfolded. While playing with our neighbour's daughter, who was roughly the same age as Abhi, both Abhi and the girl mysteriously disappeared. Mita, engaged in conversation with a woman who lived on the ground floor and was keeping an eye on the children, suddenly realized she couldn't locate

Abhi. It was early evening, and I was at my office. Around 6 PM, I received a call from my wife, informing me that Abhi had gone missing, and their search over the past hour had yielded no results. My heart sank, especially because Abhi still struggled with epilepsy, and an epileptic fit in isolation could have serious consequences.

I immediately rushed home and began searching for Abhi. Appu tirelessly scoured the neighbourhood on his bicycle, berating himself for having played cricket nearby and not keeping a closer eye on his brother. As dusk settled in, I reluctantly prepared myself to visit the local police station with Abhi's photograph, to expand the area of search with increased and professional manpower. At that moment, the mother of the woman who lived on the ground floor, a woman dealing with schizophrenia, suggested that we check inside an old Ambassador car that was rarely driven and parked in the garage. To our immense relief, we found both Abhi and the girl in the rear seat of the car. The girl had almost fainted, while Abhi was on the verge of collapsing. The oxygen levels in the closed car had almost depleted due to the carbon dioxide they breathed. Abhi, accustomed to opening the window in my Maruti car but unfamiliar with the interior of an Ambassador, had been unable to exit the vehicle. We all breathed a sigh of relief, recounting the harrowing two hours of tension that had gripped us.

Abhi, despite facing epilepsy, excelled academically and consistently ranked first in his classes. His dedication to learning and simultaneously effective management of his health condition was remarkable. Abhi's achievements earned him awards from the chief guest at school events, highlighting his resilience and commitment to education. His journey from health challenges to academic success serves as an inspiring example of determination and passion for learning.

When Abhi was just four years old, he accidentally spilt boiling milk on his entire left leg while wearing a kurta and pyjama. The scalding liquid caused the cloth to stick to his skin, resulting in immediate pain and distress. I rushed to the kitchen upon hearing his cries and quickly carried him to the bathroom, where I submerged him in cold water in a drum to alleviate the burn's effects, following the advice of medical professionals. Subsequently, I wrapped him in a warm blanket and hurried him to the family doctor.

The doctor examined Abhi's injury and administered treatment, carefully covering his entire left leg with bandages after applying a soothing and anti-burn lotion to the entire area. He emphasised the severity of the burn and the necessity for meticulous care during the dressing changes. Initially, these procedures were performed by the doctor's clinic. Later I took on the responsibility of tending to his wound at home for an extended period, approximately two months. Throughout this process, the burn gradually healed, although it left a permanent mark as a testament to Abhi's resilience and the dedicated care he received during his recovery.

Despite the burns he had suffered just a few months prior to Abhi's annual exam, he was determined to sit for it. Even though his teachers were aware of his health challenges and considering it was only a kindergarten class, they suggested waiving the annual exams considering it was only a kindergarten class, they suggested waiving his annual exams and assured him that he would be promoted to the next grade based on his outstanding performance throughout the year. However, Abhi was resolute and against the idea. Despite his burn injuries, he went ahead, took the exam papers, and emerged as the top scorer in his class.

Abhi's connection with me extended beyond these challenging moments. He cherished the times when his school was closed, and he could accompany me to my workplace. During these journeys, he would sit contentedly on my lap while I drove my car, relishing the shared moments.

In my office, he became a beloved figure, especially to one of my loyal employees, who would pamper him with a variety of soups from a nearby hotel. Abhi's presence added a sense of joy and liveliness to the workplace, brightening the days for all who interacted with him.

One remarkable memory that stands out is our journey to Badrinath, a sacred town nestled deep within the Himalayan mountains. The drive to this remote destination was no ordinary feat, particularly with young Abhi on my lap. The treacherous terrain and steep mountain roads made it a daring adventure, and our successful journey left us with unforgettable memories.

Abhi's adventurous spirit extended to our travels to Chandigarh, a city located three hundred kilometres from our residence in Gurgaon. During these trips for work, he would stay back in the hotel while I attended to my professional commitments. I would make special arrangements with the hotel staff to ensure his comfort and well-being during my absence.

One incident that exemplifies Abhi's maturity and orderliness occurred during a visit to Chandigarh. I returned to the hotel during lunchtime to find him impeccably dressed, having enjoyed a soothing bath in the bathtub. He was cosily tucked beneath a warm blanket on the bed, engrossed in watching his favourite Tom & Jerry cartoon on the television. Soft room music played in the background, creating a serene atmosphere. This episode left a profound impression on me, as it showcased Abhi's ability to handle responsibilities at such a young age.

Abhi's journey was marked by resilience, intelligence, and a loving bond with his family, creating a tapestry of memorable moments that would shape his remarkable life.

Once upon a time, in the hallowed halls of Delhi Public School, Abhi, a bright young lad in his third year of schooling, found himself in a rather peculiar situation. His closest confidant and best friend also happened to be in the same class, yet their paths diverged when it came to academics. Abhi excelled, standing tall as the unrivalled number one scholar in the entire class, earning himself a coveted place in Section A.

However, his bosom companion wasn't as fortunate in matters of the intellect. Despite possessing a heart brimming with camaraderie and a spirit eager to learn, the intricacies of academic pursuit often eluded him. Consequently, he found himself placed in Section B, a designation that created an insurmountable divide between him and Abhi.

Yearning to be reunited with his cherished friend, Abhi hatched a mischievous plan. Instead of revelling in his academic prowess, he chose to deliberately underperform in his monthly assessments. With each test, his scores dwindled, a calculated descent from the zenith of excellence he had once occupied. Slowly but surely, Abhi's cunning stratagem bore fruit.

One fateful day, after a series of lacklustre performances, Abhi's name was announced for transfer to Section B. The mischievous glint in his eye was mirrored by the knowing smile on his lips, for he had achieved his objective. No longer confined by the constraints of sectioned education, he could now comfortably sit beside his dearest companion.

This tale of Abhi's audacious manoeuvring serves as a testament to his precocious cunning, a naughtiness that blossomed from a tender age. It was a testament to his unyielding determination to bend circumstances to his will, a trait that would undoubtedly shape the course of his future endeavours. From those formative years in DPS, Abhi emerged as a young maverick, unafraid to challenge the status quo, armed with a sharp mind and a heart full of camaraderie.

In his formative years, Abhi eagerly anticipated the arrival of Mother's Day, a special occasion when he would meticulously craft heartfelt drawings to extend warm wishes of happiness and prosperity to his beloved mother.

As Abhi progressed through the ranks of his school, he achieved the esteemed position of Head Boy, a title he held for an impressive two consecutive years. This honour was bestowed upon him in recognition of his outstanding performance in his inaugural year as Head Boy. Moreover, Abhi's achievements extended beyond his school confines; he had the privilege of representing his institution at the centrally organised MUNDO, a simulation of United Nations sessions held among diverse schools from India and abroad in New Delhi every year. What makes this accomplishment particularly noteworthy is that Abhi not only had the distinction of participating in this event once, but he excelled to the extent that he was chosen to represent the school for two consecutive years, marking a significant highlight in his academic journey.

As Abhi progressed through his academic journey, I nurtured a fervent desire for him to pursue engineering at the prestigious Indian Institutes of Technology (IIT). Despite having earned my engineering degree from a different institute, I held an unwavering belief in the value of an IIT education.

When Abhi reached his tenth year of schooling, I mustered the courage to broach the subject with him. With a request laden with hope, I asked him to consider taking the joint entrance tests for the IITs. Abhi, always attuned to my aspirations, agreed, though his agreement bore traces of reluctance that I, perhaps blinded by my ambitions, failed to discern.

Recognizing the pivotal role rapid writing skills played in these entrance tests, I took it upon myself to ensure Abhi was adequately prepared. I enrolled him in a private coaching program, where he diligently attended classes after his regular school hours. In the initial stages, I would drop him off and pick him up, a routine that soon evolved as he gained independence. Abhi chose to take the bus, politely insisting that I needn't trouble myself with the commute.

It was only later, through a friend's account, that I discovered Abhi's penchant for finding solace in a quiet corner of a nearby shopping mall, leisurely sipping juice, while his coaching sessions were in full swing. Confronting him about this revelation, Abhi candidly admitted that he found the coaching sessions dull and uninspiring. Though his honesty surprised me, I refrained from coercion, opting instead to support him in his approach to preparation.

As the days dwindled to just two before the crucial admission tests, Abhi dropped a bombshell on me. He claimed to have lost his precious admit card, rendering him unable to sit for the exams. Stunned and disheartened, I sought to rectify the situation. Racing to the hallowed halls of the IIT Delhi campus, I sought an audience with the director of the joint tests, whose wife I had the privilege of knowing. However, it being a Sunday, my desperate plea for a copy of the admit card was not possible.

Abhi, regrettably, did not partake in the exams, a turn of events that left me bewildered and crestfallen. It was only later that I gleaned the truth – Abhi had engineered this situation intentionally, a strategic manoeuvre to sidestep the arduous nights of burning the proverbial midnight oil in pursuit of an engineering degree.

In the end, Abhi chose his path, diverging from the one I had envisioned. He ultimately ventured into the realm of Information Technology, carving his own niche in the R&D wing of the illustrious Daimler Group in Germany. His journey, though marked by detours and surprises, attests to the indomitable spirit of a young man who dared to forge his own destiny.

One day, as the evening sun cast long shadows on my journey back from a work trip to Faridabad, I received a call from Nanha, my nephew, who was studying engineering alongside Abhi. The news he shared was both shocking and worrisome – Abhi had taken a serious fall from a first-floor balcony while engaged in a conversation with a friend after college hours.

He was rushed to a nearby hospital with multiple injuries, especially facial. However, the local facilities in the town where he studied and resided were insufficient for his needs. Determined to secure the best care for him, Nanha swiftly transported him to the esteemed PGI hospital in Chandigarh.

Arriving at the hospital in the early hours of the morning, the sight was overwhelming. Abhi lay on a stretcher in the corridor, surrounded by other patients in various states of distress. The casualty room was teeming, occupied by those awaiting the necessary formalities before finding the final resting place of their accomplices. Abhi's face, swollen and marked by the ordeal, struck a chord of deep concern.

In his fragile state, Abhi's voice reached out, barely above a whisper. He extended an apology, expressing regret for the perceived trouble he had caused. His love and concern for me, even amidst his own suffering, moved me profoundly. Suppressing my emotions, I focused on the immediate task.

Dismayed by the limitations of the facilities and resolute in securing the best care, I embarked on the taxing journey once more, this time to a reputable hospital in Gurgaon, a five-hour drive away. Negotiating the initial administrative hurdles due to the nature of the incident, we ensured Abhi's admission. An emergency facial operation followed, during which three titanium plates were skillfully attached to his cheeks and above his right eyebrow.

After several days of intensive care, Abhi was discharged. Back at home, he embarked on a determined path to recovery. With each passing day, his strength and vitality returned. As the memory of the incident gradually faded, he resumed his studies with newfound vigour, undeterred by the challenges he had faced.

Abhi's resilience and unwavering spirit in the face of adversity left an indelible mark on our souls. His recovery became a powerful testament to the strength of the human spirit and a demonstration of the profound love that bound our hearts together. The incident reinforced the depth of our connection, and I pledged to stand by him, unwavering, through whatever trials life may present.

As time marched forward, Abhi approached his final engineering exams, a culmination of years of hard work and dedication. Meanwhile, various companies, both large and small, descended upon campuses for interviews, seeking to recruit the cream of the crop. Abhi, too, participated in this large-scale gathering of students from different colleges in Chandigarh.

After his interview, Abhi received the disheartening news that he hadn't made the cut. This news weighed heavily on him as he made the long journey back to his residence, which was approximately 150 kilometres from Chandigarh. However, upon reaching home, a phone call brought a glimmer of hope. It was Accenture, offering him a position.

Out of a staggering 15,000 hopefuls who had vied for positions during the interviews, Abhi was one of the few hundred chosen. This achievement highlighted his determination and skill. He had secured a coveted spot in this prestigious company, Accenture. From that point forward, he poured his heart and soul into his work, exceeding expectations and demonstrating his dedication.

Abhi's professional journey was marked by diligence and a pursuit of excellence. He approached each task with unwavering determination, steadily climbing the ranks within Accenture. His efforts were not overlooked, and he earned respect and recognition from both colleagues and superiors.

In the demanding world of corporate life, Abhi refined his skills, evolving from a promising young engineer into a seasoned professional. He tackled challenges head-on, showcasing his natural talent for problem-solving. Abhi's commitment and enthusiasm for his work were palpable, making him a highly valued asset to the company.

As the years passed, Abhi's achievements within Accenture stood as a testament to his strength of character and drive. His journey from a young graduate to an accomplished professional is a shining example of the rewards that await those who approach their work with dedication and passion. Abhi's story serves as an inspiration, reminding us all of the power of persistence and a commitment to excellence.

Abhi possessed not only an engineering talent but also a notable aptitude for writing. This proficiency in reading and writing was cultivated in his early years. He ventured into technical writing by contributing technical bulletins to the UK-based online magazine, Makeuseof.com. Whenever his articles were chosen for publication, Abhi received substantial remunerations in pounds. This led him to humorously remark that he was inadvertently earning foreign exchange while pursuing his engineering studies unlike me!

Abhi's interests extended beyond engineering; he had a keen eye for journalism. He even achieved a notable milestone by passing the written test for admission to a well-known institute of Journalism in Mumbai. This opportunity to dive into the world of reporting and media held a strong appeal for him. However, in a surprising turn of events, Abhi ultimately opted to join Accenture, immersing himself in technical challenges.

This decision reflected Abhi's ability to make strategic choices and seize opportunities. While journalism remained an attractive prospect, he acknowledged that his true strengths and aspirations lay in the field of technical expertise. This pivotal decision set him on a course towards a rewarding career, where his engineering proficiency would be the cornerstone of his achievements.

As September unfolds in the year 2023, there's an air of anticipation and celebration surrounding Abhi. Currently stationed in Germany, he has found a fulfilling professional niche within the esteemed Daimler Group. During the preceding summer, while he was in India, Abhi revealed his deep affection for Pankhuri Poddar. What further cemented their connection were the shared ethical beliefs and values they held dear. In light of this profound connection, they took the significant decision to unite in matrimony on the 24th of November this year, amidst the picturesque setting of Pune.

Upon hearing this joyous news, an overwhelming sense of happiness washed over all of us. In the wake of the announcement, we have found ourselves thoroughly engrossed in the meticulous planning of various facets of the forthcoming marriage ceremony. True to the couple's desires, it is to be an understated yet meaningful affair, perfectly reflecting Abhi and Pankhuri's preference for simplicity and intimacy in this special milestone of their lives.

The upcoming ceremony promises to reflect Abhi's preference for simplicity. It's a reflection of his genuine, down-to-earth nature and unassuming demeanour. Rather than an extravagant affair, the event is bound to be a heartfelt celebration of love and union, tailored to Abhi's own desires and values.

The occasion will undoubtedly be a convergence of two worlds, bringing together families, friends, and loved ones from near and far. It is a testament to the enduring bonds and connections that Abhi has fostered throughout his journey. As we approach this milestone, the air is alive with a sense of joy and excitement, as we eagerly await the union of two souls destined for a shared journey in life.

- Udayan

5

Nostalgic Treasures: From Soda Caps to Marbles, A Journey Through Childhood Hobbies

Unearthing the Rich Tapestry of Memories, One Collectible at a Time! Childhood memories are like the breadcrumbs that lead us back to who we truly are. They're the little gems of our past, each one gleaming with stories, lessons, and a whole lot of mischief. From the briefest flashes to grand affairs, they weave a tapestry of emotions and sensory overload that even a gourmet meal can't compete with.

Childhood memories are like scent-soaked postcards from the past. Whether it's the aroma of Ma's freshly baked cookies or the symphony of cricket on a summer evening, they're etched into our minds like tattoos.

These memories aren't just charming little mementoes. They're the building blocks of who we become. They're the blueprints for our coincidences, our passions, and our artistic flair. Why, I find myself rummaging through the basement of my mind, using these memories as a challenge, even now in the twilight of my days.

Ah, childhood hobbies! They're like anchors tethering us to the shores of our personal history. Sharing those tales with loved ones? It's like summoning a time-travelling caravan of nostalgia. These memories are like old vinyl records, scratchy but still playing the sweetest tunes.

Hobbies are the architects of our young minds. They're the architects responsible for building character, preferences, and skills. From building block towers to concocting culinary masterpieces, they sculpt us into the unique beings we are. They're like a self-improvement course wrapped in fun and games!

But it's not all child's play. Hobbies are like mental gyms, making us flex our cognitive muscles. Puzzles, experiments, and construction kits? They're like the boot camp for one's brain. They teach one to think, reason, and be a general know-it-all. And let's not forget the life skills they impart. Patience, attention to detail, and the sweet taste of accomplishment—they're all packed into these hobby kits

And speaking of kits, I once had a peculiar penchant for collecting soda bottle tops. Oh, the colours, the logos, the slogans! It was like a tiny pop culture museum in my room. Little did I know, I was inadvertently becoming an eco-warrior, recycling those caps before it was cool. Ah, the ignorance of youth!

Now, let's talk kites. Those graceful paper birds that once ruled the skies. They're not just pretty paper. They're cultural ambassadors, carrying the tales of far-off lands on their wings. Collecting them was like amassing a gallery of international art, each kite whispering stories of its homeland.

Ah, philately! The hobby of kings and queens, or in my case, school kids with a curious streak. Stamps and first-day covers were like passports to the world. They carried the essence of a nation in their tiny frames, and through them, I embarked on a grand tour of cultures, history, and art.

Now, let me confess my strangest collection: empty cigarette packets. These seemingly mundane packets were like time capsules of societal shifts, evolving with the times. They're an ode to design and a lesson in environmental responsibility. Who knew?

Pressed flowers and leaves were ours, meaning me and Didi, a humble attempt at botanical artistry. We'd pluck, press, and arrange them like Mother Nature's own puzzle. It was a lesson in appreciation, not just for the beauty of nature, but for the quiet marvels that often go unnoticed.

Now, let's talk ink and thread. Oh, the patterns that emerged from that fusion! It was like a dance of colours and textures, a symphony for the eyes. It taught me that creativity knows no bounds and that sometimes, the best art is the one that surprises even the artist.

And then, there were marbles. Ah, marbles! Those little spheres of history, each one a miniature masterpiece. Collecting them was like gathering fragments of time, holding the craftsmanship of bygone eras in my hands.

And finally, matchbox labels. These tiny artworks were like postcards from distant lands, each one a mini-masterpiece. They whispered stories of different cultures and eras, and through them, I travelled the world without leaving my room.

So, our childhood hobbies aren't just collections. They're windows to our past, gateways to our imagination, and bridges to our future. They're the stories we tell without uttering a word. And in cherishing them, we find a treasure trove of memories that shape us into the individuals we are today.

- Udayan

6

Harmonium Melodies: A Symphony of Memories

Notes of Nostalgia, Echoes of Music, and a Father's Melodic Legacy
I hold dear the vivid recollections of my childhood, a time when I would watch my father skillfully manoeuvring the Harmonium. It was through his renditions of bhajans and melodies, coupled with his resonant voice, that I came of age. This instrument, I dare say, played an integral role in shaping my upbringing. From the tenderest of ages, the strains of music reverberated against my eardrums, evoking an enchanting sense of the musical realm.

This particular instrument evokes a flood of nostalgic memories, with me seated, chin cradled in my hands, gazing at the Harmonium, while my father's nimble fingers danced across its keys, accompanied by his mellifluous singing. More often than not, I would reach out, caressing the instrument, running my tender hands along the bellows and reeds. Yet, permit me to offer a brief introduction to this cherished companion before I delve further.

The Harmonium, infrequently referred to as the Reed Organ, is a keyboard marvel that produces its soulful notes when wind, channelled by a hand-operated bellows, courses through a pressure-equalizing air chamber. This action sets metal reeds, fixed over apertures in metal frames, into a harmonious vibration, each within close tolerances. The pitch of the ensuing sound is determined by the size of these reeds.

The genesis of the harmonium family can be traced back to the physharmonica, conceived by Anton Haeckl in Vienna in 1818. This invention drew its inspiration from the Chinese mouth organ, introduced to Europe in the 1770s, which kindled the curiosity of certain physicists and musicians. Initially, in Europe, the bellows of the Harmonium were operated by foot, with the transition to hand-operated bellows occurring only upon their arrival in India. In

1875, Dwarkanath Ghose fashioned his rendition of the hand-pumped harmonium in Calcutta, firmly establishing its presence in Indian musical tradition. Traditionally, it accompanied Indian Classical musicians, who would often sit on the ground during performances.

My father procured his cherished Harmonium from the vibrant city of Calcutta. It was with this very instrument that he embarked on his journey of amateur singing. Gradually, his prowess garnered him numerous accolades, and I can still vividly recall watching him take the stage with it time and time again. While I never did learn to master its keys, I carry with me distinct memories of one of my brothers skillfully navigating its notes. It wasn't until later in life that I found my voice in song, but alas, without the beloved Harmonium!

- Udayan

7

Interconnectedness of Life

In this time of clash
Of civilization,
Let's cross boundaries;
Find ways and means to cross borders,
And reach out to the children's unheard voices.
Who are weak
And can't speak for themselves.
Let's reach out to the people
With value-creating education,
People with intellect and knowledge
Let's come together and reverberate
In the culture of peace
Seep into the needs of the hour
Give humanism a thought,
Culture a meaning,
Love and friendship a chance;
With humanity taking the lead.
Respecting human rights and freedom;
Respecting the need of the hour;
Let's march ahead from a culture of war
TO
A culture of love.
And the interconnectedness of life
Through human bondage and peace.

-Metali

8

The Kind-Hearted Ice Cream Maestro

A Chance Encounter with Generosity and Delight in Every Scoop

On a serene Sunday afternoon, I found myself headed to a meeting centred around the social activities I engage in during my leisure hours. With some time to spare before the rendezvous, I leisurely strolled into a nearby ice cream parlour, enticed by the prospect of savouring delectable frozen delights while idly passing the moments. To my pleasant surprise, the establishment was presided over by an elderly gentleman, well beyond the years typically associated with managing such a business venture—or so I presumed.

The parlour exuded an air of tastefulness, meticulously organized, with a petite seating area on the upper level, where patrons could indulge in their ice creams while engrossed in the glow of their laptops or engaged in intimate conversations, their voices softened in deference to the creamy delights.

An array of gastronomic pleasures stood in the enticing display within a refrigerated case, each variety bearing its name with pride. Engaging the gentleman, I learned that the shop was the brainchild of his son, who was presently occupied with other matters. In his absence, this affable elder tended to the parlour, a task he embraced with evident contentment. It is often my belief that individuals of such good-natured disposition bear no ill will in their hearts. Engaging in conversation, he briefly recounted his occupational history and how he came to manage his offspring's enterprise during his absence. Even at the cusp of eighty, he exuded a vitality that belied his years. A delightful conversationalist, he efficiently fashioned my preferred Black Currant ice cream in a crisp cone, which he promptly handed over.

Taking a more scrutinizing glance at his son's undertaking, I couldn't help but ponder over the investment it must have entailed to establish this charming parlour. After concluding my initial indulgence and opting for a second helping, this time in the form of luscious

Butterscotch, I mustered the query regarding the expenses involved in erecting and operating such a venture. He revealed that the land was his own, necessitating only the construction of the shop and the procurement of requisite machinery for the enterprise. The total expenditure tallied to ₹15 lakhs, a sum that appeared eminently reasonable given the substantial foot traffic the establishment enjoyed.

While engaged in our conversation, I inadvertently lapsed into silence, beholding an influx of increasingly youthful clientele converging as the evening gently waned. Mindful not to impose further, I took my leave, the lingering taste of the delectable ice cream still tingling on my palate.

With ample time still left before my scheduled meeting, I meandered into a nearby emporium specializing in gift articles, my intent being no more than leisurely perusal until the appointed hour drew nearer. As I perused through the various offerings, a sudden realization dawned upon me: I had departed the ice cream parlour without tendering payment. Consumed by a profound sense of chagrin, I retraced my steps with swift determination, extending my sincerest apologies to the gracious elder. Retrieving my card, I settled my debt and then inquired as to why he had refrained from summoning me back for settlement. Unperturbed, a playful gleam dancing in his eyes, he replied, 'Kind patrons always return to honour their dues.' Overwhelmed by a sense of mortification, I hastened my departure, carrying nothing but earnest prayers and well-wishes for this dear, kind-hearted old man.

- Metali

9

Whispers of March: A Day to Remember

Memoirs Etched in the Sands of Time, March 26th, 2023

On the 26th of March in the year 2023, I embarked on a new endeavour in my retired life: chronicling the memoirs of poignant moments. These words bear the unvarnished essence of my thoughts, providing a window into the current state of my mind.

Today, however, was an exceptionally remarkable day. From Stuttgart, Abhi reached out to me via a group video call alongside Appu from Mumbai, introducing me to his current and enduring sweetheart! The elation that surged through me was beyond words. For a fleeting moment, it felt almost surreal, until the weight of his revelation fully settled in, unleashing a torrent of tears. It took a while for the gravity of the moment to truly register. Later, after concluding the call, I found myself weeping even more fervently. From then on, our conversation revolved around Abhi's special lady—no, I should amend, his significant other—Pankhuri. My son, ever bashful, could only express his joy through a continuous smile while Appu detailed the evolution of their relationship. When probed about when he first became aware of their connection, Abhi revealed it had been since the previous December, during his family's visit to Germany.

In Bengali, and perhaps in Hindi as well, 'Pankhuri' translates to 'petal of a flower.' It came to light that she hails from the Marwadi community. I vaguely recollect Abhi mentioning a week-long trip to Milan, asserting it was a work-related affair. He had set off with some friends, assuring me he'd return to Stuttgart the following week. Little did I know, it was all a ruse! He now confesses that he had gone to rendezvous with this woman who had journeyed there from India on official business. When I inquired further, he explained she was a self-employed Green Energy consultant. While the particulars eluded me, I resolved to seek a more detailed account during our upcoming Saturday video call.

Abhi disclosed his plans to travel to India on the 8th of May, with a return flight scheduled for the 28th. During this time, he intends to spend a week with Pankhuri in Delhi and two weeks with us. Both my sons assured me that my long-standing desire to reunite with my brothers and sisters—one final time—will be realized when Abhi arrives. We resolved to journey to Rishikesh, where we'll rendezvous with my younger siblings and their families. Abhi will join us directly from Stuttgart via Delhi. Together, we'll spend two nights with my kin before proceeding to Lucknow to visit my elder sister, affectionately referred to as 'Danob'—a term of endearment signifying 'Ogre.' However, before delving into that, I'm eager to witness the evening 'Arati' performed by priests with illuminated lamps along the banks of the Ganges. It's an experience worth traversing a thousand miles for!

Following our sojourn at Didi's abode, we'll return to Delhi. This leg of the journey intrigues me the most. Over two days, we'll have the pleasure of meeting Pankhuri and her family, while Abhi takes on the role of introducer. I harbour a suspicion that amidst these exchanges, discussions regarding wedding dates may emerge, but I leave that thought for later contemplation.

In summary, our conversation was immensely gratifying, and now I find myself eagerly awaiting Abhi's call this upcoming Saturday to delve deeper into this captivating narrative.

Hurrah for Abhi!!! 😍😊😁😄😃😆⟨?⟩😜⟨?⟩⟨?⟩⟨?⟩

- Udayan

10

Harmony in Passing; My Short-lived Serenade

Notes of a Brief, Beautiful Melody

From the very inception of my existence, a rich tapestry of music has woven its way through the walls of my childhood home. My father, a maestro in his own right, honed his musical talents during his formative years and wielded the harmonium with remarkable dexterity. As far back as my earliest recollections, the harmonious strains of my father's voice would resonate through our abode each evening, a symphony that unfailingly touched the depths of my soul. Our household frequently played host to my father's compatriots, a congregation of kindred spirits who would join in the harmonious chorus, their melodies interwoven with the lilting notes of the tabla and the resonant strains of the sitar. Thus, it was only natural that my days unfolded to the rhythm of morning and evening melodies.

Being part of the Indian Air Force, my father found evenings largely unclaimed, allowing him to indulge in his musical pursuits. Stationed in remote camps, far removed from the clamour of urban life, we formed a close-knit community, transcending linguistic barriers. Throughout the year, our camps bore witness to celebrations infused with song and dance, a testament to the indelible spirit of camaraderie. As Bengalis, music coursed through our veins from the very cradle, an innate inclination to showcase our cultural flair at every available juncture. Thus, every camp event bore the hallmark of musical mirth. My ears grew attuned to the strains of harmonious compositions, and I eagerly anticipated these cherished evenings. In an era when television sets were a rarity and the virtual realm remained a distant dream, participating in these musical get-togethers was the pinnacle of entertainment, a cherished respite from life's rigours.

I matured into a reserved young lad, cast in the shadow of my elder sister, a mere eighteen months my senior. She personified my father's aspirations, possessing a natural effervescence that he nurtured not only in song but also in the realms of dance and dramatics. I observed with awe as she blossomed into a multifaceted woman, her talents radiating from every pore. At school, she adorned the mantle of Head Girl, immersing herself in a kaleidoscope of activities—debates, declamations, recitations, music, dance, and skits. I, content to linger on the fringes, found solace in observing rehearsals and performances from a distance, a silent admirer yearning to shed the shackles of reserve and join in the revelry.

Such was the crucible that shaped my early years, and with reluctance, I navigated my way through graduation and engineering. The reluctance stemmed from my fervent aspiration to don the uniform of the Indian Armed Forces, with dreams of becoming a fighter pilot, aspirations that, alas, remained unfulfilled. Post-engineering, I ventured forth from the comfort of my Kanpur home to Hyderabad, where I embarked on my professional journey. Throughout, I harboured a secret penchant for singing, reserving these private performances for moments of solitude, music coursing through my veins from the very inception. Yet, the thought of unveiling my talents before an audience remained a frontier I dared not traverse until a fateful turning point altered the course of my musical odyssey.

One evening, in the sanctum of my Gurgaon abode, I was greeted by two ladies, acquaintances my wife had made. Following the pleasantries, they made an audacious request: to entertain them with a song. I was taken aback, my ire directed at my wife, who had unwittingly disclosed my latent musical prowess. While I recognized the resonance of my voice, to share it openly was a proposition that bordered on the inconceivable. After their persistent entreaties, I mustered the courage to serenade them with a Tagore classic. The air was infused with soulful melodies and met with lavish praise from my unexpected audience. They implored me to visit their home the following evening, where I would be introduced to a gathering of young enthusiasts, convened to rehearse songs and dances for the upcoming Durga Puja, still two months on the horizon. There too, my efforts found resonance, dispelling the cloak of shyness that had veiled me for far too long. And so began a fleeting yet pivotal chapter in my musical journey.

Over time, I immersed myself in the rehearsals for the impending Durga Puja festivities, and with each passing day, my confidence mushroomed, the walls of silence crumbling beneath the weight of newfound self-assurance. I began to engage with fellow enthusiasts, our exchanges transcending mere melodies to encompass the broader spectrum of Bengali music and culture. My tenure at Maruti, during its nascent years in Gurgaon, demanded a herculean effort, as I toiled tirelessly, often logging in fourteen-hour days. Amidst this whirlwind, the rehearsals provided a sanctuary of solace, a balm for my weary soul. I discovered a knack for rendering the robust *manjhi* and *polli geeti* songs, renowned for their soaring pitch, a facade of my range that elevated my singing to new heights. Soon, a following began to merge around these renditions, with eager audiences flocking to witness my performances. Yet, my proficiency in the harmonium remained a glaring omission, a crutch that I leaned upon each time, reliant on another's nimble fingers to bring forth the accompanying strains. Looking back, I pondered why my father hadn't urged me to master the instrument, especially when his own musical prowess was so evident, while he fervently championed my sister's pursuits in the realm of cultural endeavours.

My musical pursuits burgeoned within the societal sphere, drawing an increasingly expansive audience captivated by my renditions. My schedule, dominated by the rigours of the factory, afforded me scant time for my young family, yet amidst the clamour of responsibility, my voice soared in harmonious rhythm. Durga Puja arrived and departed in a crescendo of celebration, with our gala performance garnering plaudits from the neighbouring community. Yet, as swiftly as it had commenced, the cycle of rehearsals and performances ground to a halt with the culmination of the Puja festivities. The subsequent year rekindled the fervour, as once again, I lost myself in the melodies. The Bengali community flourished in Gurgaon, giving rise to an array of year-round events, and my singing expanded in tandem. Gradually, my vocal prowess transcended the bounds of Gurgaon, finding resonance in nearby Delhi, where invitations beckoned us to perform at esteemed clubs. So profound was the impact of my singing that a seasoned gentleman approached me, proposing to record commercial songs in collaboration. By this juncture, I had transitioned from Maruti to embark on my own ventures, a path fraught with challenges, yet my singing endured as a sanctum of solace amid life's vicissitudes. One auspicious evening, the renowned India Habitat Centre in Delhi beckoned, a performance for the annals of memory. The event, directed by a luminary in the domain of Rabindrasangeet, happened to be the mother of a dear friend. Every day, I traversed twenty kilometres, after the demands of work, to engage in rehearsals under her astute coaching. This rigorous regimen persisted for over two months, culminating in a triumph of performance.

With each passing year, my singing continued its ascent, capturing the attention of discerning ears. Yet, my entrepreneurial pursuits, coupled with financial constraints, curtailed the trajectory of my singing career. Just as swiftly as it had unfurled, my singing ceased. One fateful night, after returning from rehearsals, an argumentative exchange with my wife transpired regarding my late arrival. At that moment, I resolved to bid adieu to the public stage, save for one final performance. Henceforth, I relinquished the spotlight, a decision that resonates through to the present day. It was then that the realization dawned—my family took precedence over all else. My wife bore the mantle of household management, steering the ship of our children's education. A dedicated educator herself, an atmosphere of scholastic diligence enveloped our home, reaping manifold benefits for our two sons. And so, I ceased to sing, dodging invitations that beckoned from all quarters. Now, at the age of sixty-nine plus, my vocal tenor remains robust. Oftentimes, I contemplate reigniting my singing endeavours, yet the flow that once surged so effortlessly has long since ebbed, and I find myself unable to rekindle the flame.

- Udayan

11

My Book Titled 'Jagat Bandhu': A Peek into My Dad's Life

Discovering the Heart Behind My Father's Journey in Life

Introduction:

"Jagat Bandhu: A Peek into My Dad's Life" is an intimate memoir that unravels the multifaceted tapestry of a beloved father's journey through the vagaries of life. Through the lens of a devoted child, this book offers a touching and insightful exploration of the experiences, values, and lessons that defined the legacy of a remarkable individual

Synopsis:

This memoir invites readers to embark on a heartfelt journey into the life of Jagat Bandhu, a man whose presence left an indelible mark on family and friends. The narrative is an affectionate tribute to a father who was not only a patriarch but also a friend, mentor, and guide. Each chapter peels back the layers of his life, painting a vivid portrait of his character, passions, and enduring influence.

From his formative years, where his dreams took root, to the challenges he overcame on the path to adulthood, the narrative chronicles the milestones that shaped Jagat Bandhu's life. It delves into his values, work ethic, and the invaluable life lessons he imparted to his family. The book celebrates the laughter, the tears, and the moments that created an unbreakable bond between father and child.

Themes:

"Jagat Bandhu: A Peek into My Dad's Life" explores universal themes of love, family, resilience, and the profound impact of parental guidance. It is a testament to the enduring influence of a father's wisdom and the enduring legacy he leaves behind.

The memoir also touches upon the passing of time, reflecting on the changing dynamics of familial relationships and the bittersweet journey of watching a parent age gracefully. It underscores the importance of cherishing every moment with loved ones.

Style and Tone:

The narrative style of the memoir is marked by its heartfelt and introspective tone. It combines personal anecdotes, family stories, and reflections to create a mosaic of memories. The prose is imbued with a deep sense of gratitude and reverence, conveying the author's love and respect for his father.

Conclusion:

"Jagat Bandhu: A Peek into My Dad's Life" is a moving tribute and a poignant exploration of the life and legacy of a cherished father. Through its heartfelt storytelling, the book offers readers a window into the profound impact of a parent's love, guidance, and unwavering support. It is a reminder to treasure the moments spent with loved ones and to honour the enduring influence of those who shape our lives.

The book is available at

Amazon (India): https://amzn.eu/d/70vxj5Z

Amazon (International): https://a.co/d/dfk7GO1

Flipkart: https://www.flipkart.com/jagat-bandhu-peek-into-my-dad-s-life/p/itm74540d7c0f752?pid=9781637546895

Pothi: https://store.pothi.com/book/udayan-banerjee-jagat-bandhu/

12

Youth, Spread Global Peace

In this world, stricken by conflict;
In this world of anxiety;
Youth! pick up the flagship
Of your gentle words,
Kind deeds, soothing voice,
Love of humanism &
Spread Global Peace.
Peace is the talk of the hour;
Peace is the need of time.
Millions of children,
In the war-stricken areas;
Beating their hearts out,
Spreading their voice.
Needs love and affection.
Rise above, the petty differences;
Cater to the needs of children;
Hear their voices;
Bring spring into their lives,
Spread the message of peace.
Let humanism, reach every corner of the world;
Spread global peace.
You are the fulcrum of society;
You are the golden pillars;
With the flagship of humanity,
Spread global peace.

-Metali

13

Bold Steps and Brave Choices

Charting a Professional Odyssey: Trials, Triumphs, and Transformation
Introduction:

"Bold Steps and Brave Choices" is a candid and vivid account of my professional journey—a trajectory that began with promise and encountered turbulent descents, yet ultimately saw a triumphant resurgence. Through this narrative, I chronicle the highs and lows, revealing the transformative power of tenacity, adaptability, and unyielding determination.

Synopsis:

The book embarks on a compelling narrative, offering readers a front-row seat to the roller-coaster ride of my professional life. It commences with the initial stages, marked by bright prospects and lofty ambitions. As the story unfolds, the narrative takes a turn, revealing the unforeseen challenges and setbacks that veiled the once-bright horizon.

With candour and introspection, I delve into the pivotal moments that ushered in the downturn in my career. The account is a testimony to the resilience demanded by such trials—moments of self-doubt, professional missteps, and the daunting prospect of forging a new path. Each chapter unveils a different facet of this tumultuous journey, shedding light on the strategies, the missteps, and the invaluable lessons learned.

Themes:

"Bold Steps and Brave Choices" explores universal themes of professional growth, resilience, and the enduring human spirit to turn the tide. It delves into the complexities of navigating a competitive landscape, offering insights into the importance of adaptability and a growth mindset.

The narrative also highlights the significance of introspection and the willingness to embrace change, even in the face of adversity. It is a testament to the transformative power of persistence and the capacity to seize control of one's destiny.

Style and Tone:

The memoir is characterized by its candid and reflective tone. It combines personal anecdotes, professional insights, and moments of self-discovery to create a narrative that is both relatable and inspiring. The prose is imbued with a sense of hope and determination, conveying the message that setbacks can serve as stepping stones to even greater success.

Conclusion:

"Bold Steps and Brave Choices" is a poignant reflection on the transformative power of perseverance in the face of professional challenges. Through its honest storytelling, the book encourages readers to embrace change, learn from setbacks, and harness their inner strength to forge a path to success. It stands as a testament to the indomitable human spirit and the capacity to overcome adversity.

The book is available at

Amazon (India): https://store.pothi.com/book/udayan-banerjee-bold-steps-and-brave-choices/

Amazon (International): https://a.co/d/aWLe3K9

Flipkart: https://www.flipkart.com/bold-steps-brave-choices-navigating-lab-life/p/itm950fbe531311c?pid=9781637547823

Pothi: https://store.pothi.com/book/udayan-banerjee-bold-steps-and-brave-choices/

14

Threads of Life: Embracing the Inevitability of Death

A Reflection on Mortality and the Resilience of the

In the tapestry of existence, we are all familiar with the inevitability of death. To some, it evokes fear, while for others, it resonates with strength and a sense of fulfilment. Life and death, akin to opposite sides of a single thread, are perspectives that shape our understanding. Those who embrace life fully harbour no fear of its eventual conclusion.

The precise moment of our departure remains shrouded in uncertainty, yet the certainty of its arrival is undeniable. What makes death tangible, even for those in denial, are the stark images of the suffering, of individuals on their final journeys. It is a truth to be accepted with rationality and grace. A wise soul once remarked, 'Life spans roughly 50-70 years of toil, born through a mother's pain and departing, leaving others in pain.'

Death, an inexorable force, shadows life as surely as night follows day, as winter succeeds autumn, and as old age follows youth. Preparations are made for the onset of winter, for the challenges of old age, yet how few ready themselves for the certainty of death, the grandest of inevitabilities.

Benjamin Franklin once wryly remarked, 'In this world, nothing can be said to be certain except death and taxes.' While taxes can be navigated with accountants or strategic living, evading death proves futile. No specialist can show us a way to dodge the inevitable, for even the most skilled physician can only delay the final reckoning. There is no corner of the earth where death does not venture. Death emerges victorious, the inevitable custodian of life itself.

To grasp the profound dance between Life and Death requires enlightenment. Education, the foundation laid as we grow, shapes every life. A well-rounded education encompasses all subjects. The years spent in college are a transformative phase, a bridge to the "real world." In youth, aspirations vary, evolving from bus driver to fighter pilot, engineer, and beyond. These were the known occupations in my surroundings. As we mature, our vision expands, revealing a myriad of potential vocations. An engineering education paved the way for the future.

Passionate about reading from a tender age, it has been a lifelong pursuit. Alas, as I near seventy, comorbidities have dimmed my focus, leading me to relinquish this cherished pastime. The melody of the song, once my forte, now emerges as a mere croak. Thus, I have turned to listening and sporadic writing.

Upon my eventual departure, I yearn for rebirth as a human, with aspirations that span across realms. As a vocalist, I dream of immersing myself in Hindustani classical music, composing and singing melodious tunes. Instruments beckon as well; the piano, guitar, tabla, and violin call out, inviting mastery. Authorship, a lifelong aspiration, envisions a library filled with non-fiction works, a testament to a lifetime of wisdom.

In the realm of sports, cricket has reigned supreme in my heart. The next life, I hope, will witness a more refined and proficient player. Alas, studies amidst challenging circumstances curtailed my pursuit of the sport.

Above all, I envision a future life marked by vibrant health, steeped in mastery of one or many of these chosen pursuits. In the grand tapestry of existence, I hope to weave a story of fulfilment, leaving footprints that transcend time itself.

- Udayan

15

Two Sisters in Harmony: A Tale of Bonds and Resilience

Sisters in Song, Strength in Unity
"Together on life's journey
We have travelled... you and me
Sharing all the joys of life
Keeping each other company.
Sharing lots of happy times
And sometimes shedding tears
Always leaning on each other
Together through the years.
And no matter where life leads us
Dear sisters know it is true
It had been a joy to travel
Down the road of life with you."

- Udayan

16

The World is Yours to Change

It's your power, it's your vision;
Your strength of mind,
Determines your attitude;
Your vision determines your ideas;
Define your perimeter of work;
Think positive, think good;
Good follows, the World is yours to Change!
It's your land,
Pure and tranquil;
Clean and heavenly, earthly;
Surrounded by good people;
You may find obstacles occasionally;
But be positive, hold hands, leave no one behind.
Be better, the World is yours to Change!
Lotus always blooms, in muddy water;
Still its beauty perceives,
In this earthly land of yours;
People enjoy their selves, at ease
keep your humanness aloft;
Always making your kind of music,
The World is yours to Change.
Be that one individual, loving and strong
With sincerity in purpose;
Loving heart,
Connect to all,
Especially the weak,
Keep your baton high,
Forging connections through your voice
The world is yours to change.
Be the voice of love,

Be the voice of friendship,
Enjoy together in your communities,
In your land,
Forging ahead, with love and faith,
With the flagship of confidence;
The world is yours to change.
Let your utterances
captivate all;
Forge ahead with devotion
And sincerity;
Connecting everyone;
Learning from precious writings,
Learning from their experience;
The world is yours to change
The need of the hour is peace,
Equality and comradeship,
Harnessing your learning
Marching ahead with confidence
sharing your learning,
Even if you can enlighten one single person
The world is yours to change.
Knowledge is not intellectual right;
The more you share, the more you grow;
Learn together, grow together;
Playfully, lovingly, share and grow
The world is yours to change.

17

Memories Woven in Time: A Tribute to My Grandmother

Stitched in Time, Treasured Forever

During my childhood, visiting my grandmother's house was always a magical experience. The outhouse was a haven of greenery, with the vibrant morning sun, fragrant blooms, cheerful birdsong, and the gentle caress of the breeze creating an enchanting symphony. Dewdrops adorned the leaves like glistening jewels, while butterflies danced amidst the flowers. Among them, the *shiuli* flowers with their striking orange stems held a special allure. They carpeted the ground around their tree, infusing the air with their sweet, lingering fragrance.

Armed with a bamboo wicker basket, I would set out to gather *shiuli*, roses, lilies, marigolds, lotus, and an array of other blossoms. With nimble fingers, I would weave them into exquisite garlands for my dear granny, who cherished them for her daily rituals and poojas. Each flower in those garlands possessed a unique beauty, much like how grapes, apples, and guavas each carry their own distinct identity. A garland, though an amalgamation of many flowers, possessed its singular charm, showcasing the unity and splendour of nature.

My grandmother, with her boundless wisdom, imparted invaluable lessons about the individuality of each flower. She illustrated how they differed in fragrance, sweetness, and colour, emphasizing the importance of recognizing and respecting the distinctiveness of every person. This wisdom became a guiding light for me, especially after the loss of my parents at a tender age.

As life unfolded, I was blessed to forge deep connections with some extraordinary friends. One of them, a cherished companion of over a decade, gifted me two spacious glass fishbowls adorned with flourishing ivies nestled amidst soil and pebbles. These became a source of pride in my living space, adorning the windowsill. They breathed life into the morning light, casting a refreshing aura. Anyone who visited our home couldn't help but be captivated by the ivies, which thrived abundantly along the large ledge in my living room. They became a topic of animated discussion within our family, symbolizing growth and vitality, much like the expanding branches of our family tree.

Then, the unforeseen occurred. This morning, my brother accidentally broke the bowls while cleaning them. The delicate glass, fragile by nature, could not withstand the unintended force. I was stunned, my heart sinking. I grappled with a storm of emotions, imagining all the possible misfortunes that might befall my brother due to this inadvertent act. However, my grandmother's voice echoed in my mind, whispering, "Whatever happens, happens for good. Focus on the half of the tumbler that's filled with water, not the empty half filled with air."

I took a moment to reflect and realized that the beauty of those ivies had already brought immense joy to my family. It had enabled us to replace the fishbowls, this time with clear acrylic ones that promised durability. With my grandmother's wisdom as my anchor, I scoured e-commerce sites for these unbreakable acrylic fishbowls adorned with ivies. To my delight, I found a plethora of stunning options to choose from. Swiftly, I placed an order for a couple of them, settling back with a sense of satisfaction. Despite the day's rocky start, I knew it was within our power to turn it around into a day filled with smiles and promise.

- Metali

18

Sumati: The Beacon of Abhi's Early Education

Guiding Light Through Abhi's Educational Journey

When Neeta's child arrived prematurely, it marked the beginning of a three-year sabbatical from her workplace. During this time, she devoted herself entirely to her baby's development, striving to ensure he met milestones akin to his peers. The initial year proved to be a strenuous trial; the baby's constant awakenings for feeds left Neeta sleep-deprived and drained. Mornings brought the added responsibility of seeing off her elder child to school, as her husband's assistance was limited. The toll on her health was evident, with puffy eyes serving as a testament to the sacrifices she made. Despite these challenges, Neeta found solace in the paediatrician's delight at her child's progress.

Neeta invested in a myriad of games designed to stimulate her child's various faculties. She meticulously tailored meals to his preferences and took him to the park for activities that honed his skills and abilities.

Books were procured to refine his motor skills, while evenings were filled with playful visits to the modern park near their home. It was equipped with an array of games and activities that bolstered his communication, interaction, and even musical aptitude. Observing her child's development was an ongoing source of joy and pride for Neeta.

When he was eventually admitted to a well-reputed school, he excelled, securing a spot among thousands of students. The school's principal generously permitted Neeta to stay on the premises, allowing her to witness her child's growth in their nurturing environment. Under the guidance of Sumati, a compassionate teacher, he flourished academically and emotionally. Sumati's dedication extended beyond the classroom; she provided the comfort and support he needed to navigate his emotions, especially when met with frustration.

Part teacher, part mentor, and part friend, Sumati played a pivotal role in shaping the child's early educational experience. His participation in a drawing competition resulted in him clinching the first position across all schools in the city, instilling a newfound confidence and enthusiasm for school activities.

Neeta expressed her gratitude to Sumati through gestures, often bringing flowers. However, she knew that no gift could adequately convey the depth of her appreciation for Sumati's love, kindness, and unwavering support. Sumati occasionally bent the rules, allowing the child to borrow toys, books, and DVDs from the school, always with the understanding that they would be returned promptly.

As Neeta looked back on those cherished years, she realized she had lost touch with Sumati and regretted not preserving her contact information. Although Neeta was naturally outgoing, she couldn't forgive herself for not staying connected with such a remarkable woman who had been a guiding light for her child. She resolved that during her next visit to Gurgaon, she would embark on a search to reunite with this exceptional soul who had played the role of godmother, friend, teacher, and benefactor to her child. In her heart, Neeta wished for educators everywhere to possess the same compassion and devotion she had witnessed in Sumati.

- Metali

19

Journey of Resilience: A Tale of Survival and Generosity

A Traveller's Odyssey Through Trials and Unexpected Acts of Kindness
The year was 2003 or 2004. I don't clearly remember. I was to go on a longish tour of Italy and England. First I was to fly to Milan from where I was to take a train to Perugia, which is about five hours away with one change at Florence. There I was to be joined by my MD for a meeting with an important client for disc brake pads. After the meeting the next day, we were to travel to Rome by train, stay the night there, and board a flight for Heathrow in London the next morning. After a series of meetings at Southampton, Manchester, Leeds and Coventry spanning three days, I was to travel singly to Heathrow for a flight the next morning back to Milan, and onwards to Nardò for continuation of disc brake pads testing and getting certification as per ECE norms. There I was to stay for a week before taking a flight back home via Malpensa.

So far so good. But the tour started on a bad note. The night I was to fly out from Delhi at 1:30 the next morning, I returned home very late from my office and hurriedly packed my things into my favourite suitcase and crammed my office trolley bag with whatnot. I wasn't feeling very well and somehow ate whatever my wife forced me to have in between my packing. I stuffed the forex I had for the trip into my purse and stuck it into the inside pocket of my blue blazer. I usually distribute the forex I carry in at least three places – my blazer, my suitcase and my office bag – so that if by chance lose one, I have the others for a backup. But that night I kept all of it, about €750, in one place – my purse – despite my wife reminding me again and again to distribute the money into three places. But I was in a hurry as otherwise I might miss my flight. Besides the euros, I had about ₹2,000 too in my purse.

Giving my wife a hasty hug and a peck on the cheek, and kissing my sonnies goodbye, I rushed out to board my car to the airport. Of course all the time I wasn't feeling well at all and felt it worsening with time. I tried but couldn't place a finger on why it was happening. Anyhow I reached the airport and after a quick check-in, immigration and security, I slumped onto a seat at the waiting lounge near my boarding gate. Quickly I semi-dosed off and anxiously waited for my flight's departure to be announced.

Onboarding, I slid down onto my seat at the window and waited patiently for the flight to take off so that I could down a couple of neat scotches and drift away to sleep. After a time the stewardess woke me up from my light slumber to offer me a drink of my choice, but I decided not to go ahead with my customary scotch and skipped my in-flight meals too.

Since the flight was a Lufthansa one, it landed in Frankfurt, where a famished me took the connecting flight to Malpensa. I felt a lot better in the morning but skipped my breakfast on the flight thinking of having a sumptuous breakfast of my choice at Milan Central railway station at my favourite eating joint in the station. This was about an hour from Malpensa by bus and by the time I reached there I was almost tripping over myself with an empty stomach. Added to that was the urgent need to pass urine. The toilet was at the other end of the massive station and I thought of going there after I purchased my train ticket for Perugia. I quickly purchased the ticket and hurried towards the urinal with my bladder almost bursting. Added to my woes, was my luggage, though on wheels.

Upon reaching the large urinal, I was halted at the automatic gate for a permit to use the toilet which could be purchased there. I reached into the inside of my blazer to retrieve my purse and soon was holding the 'prized' billet in my hand. Shoving it into the slot, I rushed in to relieve myself, which I did with a lot of satisfaction and joy. I looked around and found the janitor, who was cleaning the floor and who had helped me purchase the ticket, giving me a thumbs-up sign. Acknowledging his sign, I hurried out to my favourite eating joint on the promenade leading to the platforms. Reaching the restaurant, I was joyfully greeted by a loud 'Bon Giorno', which, as you guessed correctly meant 'good morning', by the sweet girl serving the guests. Since I was a regular there, I ordered my usual breakfast and reached inside my blazer pocket for the purse to make payment.

It wasn't there! I checked the other pocket, and it wasn't there either. With my heart beating fast, I rushed out and almost ran to the toilet and searched around thinking it had fallen somewhere. Immediately the janitor came rushing forward and kept on asking me in Italian if I had lost something. In a harsh tone, I told him that he had taken my purse or was in knowledge of its whereabouts. But he touched his heart and tugged at his throat, which is customary amongst Italians when they have to swear, indicating he didn't have any knowledge of it.

Crestfallen and exasperated, I forgot all about my hunger and started looking for a police post to file my complaint. I had last eaten a light lunch the previous day at my factory and later a hurried small mouthful at home before boarding my car for the airport. How I longed for a cigarette then! I was a habitual smoker then and used to smoke about fifty of them on average every day. The last I smoked was before boarding the flight and I then thought of buying my pack of cigarettes at the Milan train station. I dug my hand into my pockets only to come out empty every time. And then I remembered I hadn't a cent on me, whether to buy a cigarette or have my breakfast. Totally despondent, I trudged towards platform one where I was told the police post existed. It was fairly a big one, but I could see a longish line of about nine people, all foreigners and all women. A cop sat at a desk at the end of the line and replied to the first complainant with gestures, shrugging his shoulders and pushing up his palms upwards, as is with Italians when they are agitated. The woman was clearly very flustered and wildly gesticulating by flailing her arms in gay abandon, which had a minimalist effect on the cop. After twenty minutes or so, and after the first woman in question, didn't seem to be satisfied, I decided to give seeing the police officer a miss since waiting in the line to see him would surely make me miss my train which was another half an hour away. So I did the next best thing I could think of and settled down on a bench on the platform from which my train was to depart, to start ringing my contacts in Milan for some money so that I could eat something and reach Perugia. Once there I could borrow money from my MD and proceed further. Credit cards were not as common in those days as now and moreover, I didn't have one then.

Settling down on a bench, I first rang up Simone, my friend from Piacenza, an industrial city about 80 km south of Milan. I was to request him to ask any of his friends in Milan to come to the station and give me some money. But to my bad luck, Simone was away to the UK on business. He was with a hydraulic press manufacturing company and used to sell their products globally. Simone was very sorry when he understood my plight and promised to call back with some good news after calling his friends in Milan. His call came back some twenty minutes later to say he tried contacting three of his friends, all of whom said they would take at least a couple of hours to reach the station. He proceeded to ask me to take the next train which was some four hours later. I thought about it and decided not to cancel this train as I was sure to get the money from my friend from Naples, Rosario, who could ring up anyone of his contacts to deliver a certain amount to me when I changed trains at Florence. Rosario was very well-connected politically and his father, Corrado Sr, was someone important in their parliament. I was so sure to get funds through him that I hurriedly bade goodbye to Simone and dialled Rosario.

The line was totally blank. I called several times and every time I was disappointed. I was so desperate with hunger and the bad itch to smoke, that I almost tore my hair out. My train backed up onto the platform and, with a heavy heart, I boarded the train, dreading the five hours of journey ahead till I reached my hotel in Perugia. The train had just started to inch out of the station when suddenly I got a ring on my mobile. It was Rosario! Excitedly I connected but the line went dead. What luck! I tried to ring back but with the same result. After half an hour, I got his phone again and this time the line didn't go blank. On hearing that I was in Italy, he excitedly asked me where I was and when I was going to see him in Naples. Rosario knew that I used to frequent Nardò regularly for testing the brake pads and also had once visited him by journeying by bus from Lecce to Naples through the mountainous and snowy Potenza. But before I could tell him about my predicament, the train entered the many tunnels that came on the way and I lost connection. Come as it may, I couldn't connect with him again later.

Florence came and I continued on my journey after changing trains there. The food trolleys came and went and the only thing I could do was stare at them, all the time wishing I had some change kept in my blazer pocket. Clutching my stomach and craving for a smoke, I whiled away my time observing this and that. About an hour from Perugia, I chanced upon a teenager who was going about on the train distributing some pamphlets. Eventually, he came to me and handed me one such leaflet. On it was the picture of the Virgin Mary with the infant Jesus on her lap and a request written there to help the teenager in question with as much money as anyone could. Claiming he was a Ukrainian refugee, he requested passengers to help him with whatever money they could so that he could pursue his higher studies in Perugia. Here I must apprise my readers of the fact that Perugia is known for Engineering and other professional studies in Italy. When this guy came to me, I excused myself describing my events since morning and that I was extremely hungry then. Surprisingly he offered me Euro 20 from his collections from various passengers saying I could purchase some food with it and that I could return the amount later when and if I so desired. I was overwhelmed with emotions and thanked the guy for his generosity and told him that I would disembark at Perugia which was about fifteen minutes away, and that I would satisfy my hunger at the hotel where I would check in for the night.

Alighting at Perugia, I looked for the vehicle from the hotel which would come to collect me from the station. The hotel was about half an hour away and I reached there at about five in the evening. Exhausted, exasperated and hungry, I literally dragged myself to the check-in counter and asked for some food. The lady at the counter was aghast to see my state but couldn't give me anything to eat as the restaurants were closed then. But she said she could whip up some hot chocolate drink and the room I checked into had some cookies and aerated drinks in the fridge there. I thanked her and soon I was gladly sipping on the hot chocolate drink and munching away on some much-needed cookies and fruits the room offered.

With something in my stomach, I dosed off to a deep slumber to dream about that teenage 'beggar' on the train whose behaviour deeply impressed me. I was reminded that though different from different countries and backgrounds, we are eventually one. Human emotions run the same way worldwide. At the end of the day, it's humanism which engulfs all of us across all continents with love and warmth!

- Udayan

20

Twist of Fate: A Narrow Escape on July 7th, 2005

A Journey Disrupted, a Flight Missed, and a Life Spared by an Unexpected Turn of Events

In the company of our friend Danielle Bendandi, who kindly dropped us off at Rome's Fiumicino International Airport, Mita and I bid farewell to him, along with Irene and their child. As we ventured inside to complete our check-in and other necessary formalities, a sense of yearning for the comfort of home after an exhausting ten-day journey washed over us. With the paperwork done, we found our seats, anticipating the announcement of our flight. Soon enough, the announcement came, and we boarded. Our initial destination was Munich, where we were to catch a connecting flight back to Delhi.

We settled into our seats, awaiting the completion of the aircraft's pre-flight procedures and the subsequent departure for Munich. However, time seemed to stretch on without any movement. The captain informed us that an accident involving a police helicopter had occurred on the runway, causing a delay. We were assured that we would take off once the runway was cleared. As minutes turned into hours, it became evident that we would miss our connecting flight to Munich. Both of us were disheartened, particularly as our younger son had fallen ill and we were eager to return promptly.

Taking matters into my own hands, I approached one of the counters and requested the attendant to book us on the next available flight to Delhi. Regrettably, she informed us that no earlier flights were accessible. There was, however, an earlier flight departing from Heathrow. She suggested booking us on a flight to London early the next morning, from where we could catch a connecting flight to Delhi. Considering the eight-hour layover at Heathrow after our arrival at eight in the morning, I contemplated taking the tube to King's Cross.

There, we could rendezvous with a couple of friends before returning to the airport in the afternoon to continue our journey back home. My wife agreed with the plan, and the attendant proceeded to book us on that flight.

The girl at the desk was about to book us on the flight when she said there was an earlier flight which left from Frankfurt the next afternoon but the seats were differently numbered and we would have to request the air hostess after boarding to put us adjacent to each other if it was possible. I said that was okay with me and she booked us on that flight.

Subsequently, we were transported to the nearby Hilton Hotel to spend the night. Our flight to Frankfurt was scheduled for the next morning at eleven. Although we were disappointed not to reach home sooner, we made the best of our stay at the hotel. The following morning, we awoke, got ready, and descended to the dining area for breakfast. After a satisfying meal, I settled into a nearby lounge with a cup of coffee, watching the news broadcast on the large screen before me. The breaking news was a terror attack on the metro at King's Cross, which occurred at precisely nine in the morning, during the peak of the morning commute. The devastating incident claimed numerous lives, with additional incidents taking place at various locations in London.

The gravity of the situation struck me like a thunderbolt! Both Mita and I were slated to be at King's Cross station precisely at the same time as the detonation if we had opted for the flight from Heathrow. It was a twist of fate that intervened. What a narrow escape! I rushed to the reception counter, called my wife, and shared the news. She was left speechless, offering prayers of gratitude for our miraculous deliverance from imminent disaster. This unforgettable day, July 7th, 2005, is forever etched in my memory!

- Udayan

21

Jog Falls: Nature's Symphony of Cascading Waters

*Where Water Defies Obstacles, Painting a Canvas of Vibrant Hues,
Uniting Hearts Across Borders*

Jog Falls, India -
what a view of water cascading down,
amongst all hurdles
making its way
for itself.
The sunrise shining and spreading
Radiance along its path.
The Victoria Falls,
the Niagara
All captivates and quenches the mind & thoughts of
The love of all tourists.
Water so life-giving and endearing.
We any country, any place, are joined by water.
Join in the human chain of love and compassion
Standing by the falls
In the evening
Light breeze from over the water
A myriad of colours,
Color the environment.
Then my Sari drape was pulled
By a girl inquiring is it dark?
I replied it's twilight,
light is at the end of the tunnel.

- Metali

22

From Naïvete to Mastery: A Journey of Engineering and Leadership

Navigating Financial Constraints, Embracing Challenges, and Pioneering Change in the Indian Automotive Industry

Embarking on the journey of obtaining my Engineering degree was no small feat, particularly when it came to financial constraints. Having graduated in Science from a prestigious institution in Kanpur, I was acutely aware of the strain on my father's finances. He, a man already grappling with economic hardships, made it explicitly clear that he couldn't shoulder any additional burdens for my education. It was evident to me, albeit unspoken, that he harboured a deep desire for me to pursue further studies, even though his heart shattered as he uttered those words. This sentiment was further underscored by his reluctance to suggest I seek employment, despite his own ongoing professional commitments. He could have urged me to work and contribute to my younger siblings' education and my elder sister's wedding, thus lessening his financial burden. Yet, he refrained from doing so.

In turn, I mustered the courage to entreat him to permit me to pursue Engineering, confident that I could cover the costs through scholarships. When I broached this subject, a glint of pride and hope sparkled in his eyes, and he encouraged me to forge ahead. Thus, I secured admission into a renowned engineering institution and dove into my studies with unwavering determination.

The financial strain, however, remained palpable. Acquiring the expensive textbooks necessary for my coursework proved to be a daunting challenge with my modest scholarship funds. Moreover, I couldn't afford to reside in any of the three hostels available. Instead, I embarked on a daily 21-kilometre bicycle journey to reach the college, regardless of the bitter cold of winter, the buffeting winds, the pouring rain, or scorching summer temperatures. Each day, I would arrive at the college by 7 a.m., finding solace in a meticulously organized library, diligently taking notes and studying until my first class commenced at 9 a.m. This arduous routine was unyielding, spanning even the most inclement weather conditions. I would leave my home at the crack of dawn, navigating through the elements to reach the college, unfailingly. Post-classes, I would often engage in rigorous sports activities, particularly cricket, on the college grounds, reserving exceptions for days when laboratory work took precedence. Predictably, I would be utterly exhausted by day's end, yet unwaveringly committed to completing my assignments and studies, often retiring late into the night, only to rise again at the break of dawn.

On weekends, my mother would rise early to prepare a modest breakfast. She would pack two chapatis accompanied by pickles in a newspaper, for me to carry in the back pocket of my trousers, ensuring I had sustenance for lunch, which I would relish with a steaming cup of tea in the college canteen.

This rigorous routine persisted for four long years, culminating in the gratifying moment of donning the graduation robes and receiving my hard-earned engineering degree at the college convocation. Simultaneously, I clinched a promising position in Hyderabad, thanks to the company's campus recruitment policy.

At that juncture, my father was stationed at the Indian Air Force base in Srinagar, grappling with an ear ailment that necessitated surgery at the Army Base Hospital in New Delhi. After my final interview at the company's headquarters in Delhi, I hastened to the hospital, braving the rain-soaked streets. There, amidst the barracks' verandah, I spotted my father, patiently waiting for me. Ignoring my wet clothes, he enveloped me in a tight embrace, planting a warm kiss on my cheek. Even now, at the age of 69, that moment remains etched in my memory, as vivid as if it transpired just yesterday. In his eyes, I detected a glistening hint of a tear.

Shortly thereafter, I set off for Hyderabad, ready to embark on this new chapter. While excitement coursed through me, a tinge of sorrow accompanied me, knowing I was leaving behind my entire family in Kanpur, with whom I had shared every moment of my life until then. The company was reputable and compensated well by industry standards, yet I commenced as a trainee engineer, drawing a modest salary of ₹800 per month. This was the year 1978, and though the remuneration seemed meagre, it sufficed for me to secure a small one-bedroom rental and dine at a nearby eatery. Work-life was demanding, thrusting me into the maelstrom of corporate politics and gruelling physical labour. The company was notorious for its unyielding approach to training its executives, and though exasperated at times, I later recognized the fortitude it instilled in me, underpinning my later career endeavours.

As the years rolled by, I weathered numerous challenges, learning to surmount them through a blend of skill, ingenuity, and sheer determination. I forged valuable friendships, primarily within the company, and life took on a steady rhythm. Yet, one lesson proved elusive—the art of prudence in pivotal decisions that would impact my personal life. Raised by my parents to be diligent, earnest, and devoted, I matured into a somewhat reticent young man when confronted with choices that bore weight on my contentment. I was willing to make sacrifices, readily offering up my own happiness for the sake of the company and others, within my capabilities. It wasn't until much later in life that I came to rue this inclination, a realization that dawned a tad too late.

Diligence in the company bore fruit, and I ascended the ranks, securing three promotions in as many years following my two-year training period. Swiftly, I ascended to the position of department manager, actively engaging in high-level managerial deliberations. More often than not, my insights found their way into pivotal management decisions.

Before long, my reputation reverberated throughout the country in my field of engineering. Professionals from diverse industries extended feelers, discreetly gauging my interest in joining their ranks. Their overtures were veiled, presuming I might be disenchanted with my current position and open to a change. Noteworthy among these were offers from Tata Motors Ltd. and Eicher Motors Ltd., both of which I entertained. In my heart, I knew I wouldn't like to bid farewell to my current role, yet a new opportunity presented itself, knocking at my door.

In 1982, a call from the Vice Chairman and Managing Director of Maruti Udyog Limited altered the course of my professional trajectory. This project, backed by the Indian government, entailed the establishment of a small car manufacturing unit in technical and commercial collaboration with Suzuki Motors Ltd., Japan, in Gurgaon (now Gurugram). It was an endeavour of considerable prestige and promise. With an open plane ticket in hand, I was summoned to Delhi, where I was to meet with them to discuss my potential role in this monumental project. The gravity of the situation weighed heavily on me, for I was in a state of flux, both professionally and personally. This was compounded by the fact that I had married just a year prior in July, and my wife was expecting our first child. A month later, on December 10, 1982, we welcomed a radiant, smiling boy into the world. Only after his arrival did I set out for Delhi, a decision that held a significant bearing on the trajectory of my life.

- Udayan

23

Journey of Resilience: From Naïvete to Industry Pioneer

Navigating Career Challenges, Embracing Change, and Pioneering Automotive History in India

I named these pivotal phases of my life and career "Naïveté" for a reason. In my formative years, I poured my heart and soul into my work, prioritizing my job over personal gains. This trend continued even after marriage and the birth of my son. I was too inexperienced to strike a balance between my professional and personal life, a shortcoming that left me oblivious to life's intricacies. I often placed unwarranted trust in people, failing to discern their true intentions. This trait, unfortunately, did not serve me well as I progressed in both my career and personal life.

Yet, despite the comfort and stability offered by my position in Hyderabad, I resolved to leave and embrace the challenges of a new role in Gurgaon. However, I chose to embark on this new endeavour alone initially, so as not to disrupt my sister-in-law and brother-in-law's studies, both of whom had come to live with us after the untimely passing of my parents-in-law.

Upon much contemplation, I submitted my resignation. Predictably, my initial attempt was met with resistance; my resignation letter was summarily rejected. General Manager summoned me to his office, insisting that I continue as before. My performance had been exemplary, earning me three promotions in as many years—an unprecedented feat in those times. The GM assured me of further advancements and a substantial increase in salary and benefits in the following year. The allure of these incentives was undeniable, tempting me to retract my resignation and remain in my current position. Nevertheless, the desire to acquire new knowledge, combined with Mr. Krishnamurthy's compelling vision, ultimately led me to take the courageous step of launching a lucrative career with the new auto company in Gurgaon.

I patiently waited for a week for the management to accept my resignation, but it never transpired. Faced with this impasse, I made the decision to leave the company and join the new one in Gurgaon. I planned to return later to bring my wife and newborn child. Additionally, I needed to ensure my sister-in-law was settled with her aunt in Hyderabad, and my brother-in-law, a first-year college student, had suitable accommodation to continue his studies before joining us in Gurgaon.

With a modest bundle of belongings, I boarded a train bound for Gurgaon. At that time, Gurgaon was far from the bustling city it is today. It was more akin to a village, surrounded by tall elephant grass, with only sparse dwellings dotting the landscape. After a bit of searching, I managed to secure a rented place in Sector 4. From there, I made my way to the address specified in my appointment letter to join the new company.

The factory, situated on elevated terrain, was the brainchild of the late Sanjay Gandhi, the younger son of Indira Gandhi, and the driving force behind the joint venture's inception. However, the project had been shrouded in controversy, as the land acquisition process had faced opposition from local communities. When I arrived, the factory was still in its infancy, with only a handful of employees. I was the sixth engineer to join, though there were staff members in other departments such as accounts and personnel. Given the Public Sector nature of the enterprise, civil engineering activities were managed by experts from various national organizations. The entire project, from design to execution, had been entrusted to Mecon India, headquartered in Ranchi. They operated from a small building which formerly housed Sanjay's car plant's tool room.

In this setting, I presented my joining letter to the General Manager. However, he requested a release letter from my former company, which I couldn't produce, having essentially fled from it. The GM informed me that joining without this document was a non-negotiable requirement due to the Public Sector nature of the company. Stuck in this predicament, I weighed my options. Returning to request the release letter seemed futile, as I anticipated it would likely be denied. Caught between a rock and a hard place, a sudden idea struck me. The following day, I visited my company's head office, located in close proximity to the new company's headquarters where I had been interviewed. There, I met a gentleman named Shinh, the executive director of the company. Despite his youthful demeanour, he held grand plans for my advancement within the company. When I explained my situation, he advised me to return to Hyderabad, assuring me that he would travel there in a few days. Once there, he would discuss my case with senior management. So, I returned to Hyderabad and awaited the ED's arrival, which occurred within the week.

In a meeting that spanned an entire day, the ED gathered with numerous other company executives, primarily senior figures. We delved into a range of issues, spanning finance to manufacturing. At times, he even sought my input, as if my resignation hadn't even transpired. When lunchtime arrived, we adjourned to a nearby room, avoiding discussions of business matters and instead engaging in candid conversations about various personal matters. After a sumptuous meal, we reconvened in the meeting room to conclude the day's proceedings. Around seven in the evening, after many had already left, the ED addressed my resignation letter. He inquired about the job opportunity that enticed me enough to leave my current position. I provided a comprehensive explanation, emphasizing my keenness to acquire new skills. After extensive deliberation, he accepted my letter and extended his well-wishes. Additionally, he waived my three-month notice period, encouraging me to return to the company if needed, on my own terms. I expressed my heartfelt gratitude and turned my attention to arranging my wife's and child's relocation to Gurgaon, as well as securing suitable accommodations and arrangements for my sister-in-law and brother-in-law.

In early January 1983, the chilling cold greeted us as our train pulled into Delhi station at dawn. Clasping our son, Appu, in a warm embrace, Mita cradled him close to her chest to shield him from the bitter cold. We boarded a taxi, which could only take us up to the Delhi-Haryana border due to an odd rule at the time. For reasons unknown, cabs from Delhi required an expensive permit to enter Haryana. At the border, we transferred to an autorickshaw, which ferried us to sector seven, where I had already secured a rental home. As our belongings were en route via truck, we lacked any furnishings for our new abode. Fortunately, our landlord generously provided us with mattresses, duvets, and bedsheets, allowing us to fashion a comfortable bed on the floor. It was a night of finding respite from the biting cold. The next priority was arranging for sustenance.

During those times, Gurgaon was far from the bustling metropolis it would become. It resembled more of a sleepy village in Haryana, rich in historical significance. Tall grasses swayed in the breeze, and dining establishments were a rarity. I identified a dhaba (a local eatery) near our house and negotiated with the proprietor to pack our meals, which a neighbouring paan shop owner, Harish, would deliver to our doorstep daily. In the evenings, I would fetch them myself. I am eternally grateful for Harish's assistance, from whom I also purchased cigarettes, bread, and butter for breakfast. In due time, I retrieved my motorcycle from the station, ensuring it would be loaded onto the same train I would be taking to collect it in Delhi the following day.

With my family comfortably settled in our new home, I embarked on my motorcycle to join Maruti Udyog Limited. Armed with my release letter from the previous company, my induction into the new role progressed seamlessly. It was then that I learned I was the sixth engineer to join the Gurgaon project!

In a room slightly smaller than a hall, all eighteen of us convened. This included senior personnel from Mecon Industry, Ranchi, who would oversee construction activities within the company. In a matter of days, we were slated to undergo an intensive training program at Suzuki Motor Corporation in Japan. The program was slated for 100 days, and we were initially introduced to basic Japanese language instruction. This language, notoriously challenging, presented a slow learning curve. However, within a few months, we were ready to embark on our journey to Japan. Media coverage of our departure coincided with political upheaval in the country. Many argued that the project was driven by political motives and doubted Mrs Gandhi's ability to see it through. I had to carefully plan for my wife and Appu's stay during the next 100 days until my return. Communication was a considerable challenge during those times, so precision in planning was paramount. With all my belongings in tow, which had arrived later by truck, I confirmed that the house was set up to our satisfaction.

Before long, we departed for Japan, a distant land renowned for its technological advancements and management practices. Our journey took us from New Delhi to Hong Kong and then to Osaka, Japan. Everywhere we went, we were treated with exceptional warmth and hospitality, be it at the airport or in a store. It was widely known in Osaka and Japan that we were guests of the Japanese Government, as we were the individuals slated to be trained and then return to implement not only the technology but also the acclaimed management methodologies in India. Our training began at Kansai Kensu Centa, where we were provided individual rooms for language learning. We attended classes every morning and, after lunch, our teacher would take us out to practice conversing with locals at stores and in public spaces. The warmth and affection extended to us left a lasting impression. This routine continued, and gradually but surely, we began to understand the Japanese way of life. We also took part in weekly lectures delivered by experts from Japanese universities, including a Nobel Laureate.

After about forty-five days of such training, we embarked on a tour of Western Japan, travelling by bus and train. By this time, we were proficient enough in the Japanese language to engage in conversations. We visited Himeji, Kobe, Nagasaki, Hiroshima, and several other towns and cities. We also had the opportunity to witness the craftsmanship of a pottery-making factory, which left us awestruck by the precision and discipline exhibited by the local artisans. However, visiting Hiroshima and Nagasaki was a somber experience, as we witnessed the aftermath of man's cruelty to his fellow humans. The scenes in those cities were heart-wrenching.

Following our week-long excursion, we returned to our hostel. Before long, it was time for a farewell party, and we bid farewell to Kansai to begin our technical and managerial training in Hamamatsu. The location of our hostel, perched on a hill overlooking the Pacific Ocean, offered a breathtaking backdrop. Here, we plunged into an intensive eight-week training program focused on small car manufacturing. It was an arduous undertaking, but we emerged with a comprehensive understanding of the entire process, from production to setting up an industry.

Soon, our training came to a close, and we were transferred to Tokyo Kensu Centa, where we spent three nights before bidding farewell to a country that had risen from the ashes of a devastating war to become a global powerhouse in just thirty years. We returned home via Bangkok, ready to implement what we had learned and establish a small car factory in India, with an emphasis on mass production for the middle-income demographic. What we accomplished went on to make history.

- Udayan

24

Mita's Grand Adventure: A Comedy of Travel Obsessions and Dreaming Big

Broke, But Never Broken. Join Mita on a Journey of Wanderlust, Laughter and Unstoppable Dreams!

Ah, the tale of my marriage to Mita, a whirlwind romance that began in 1981. Picture it: She was a sprightly 19-year-old with a zest for life, and I was...well, let's just say I had a full head of hair back then.

Now, I won't lie, our journey together has been like a roller coaster. But not the exciting, scream-inducing kind. No, ours was more like a rusty old Ferris wheel that occasionally got stuck at the top. We've had more downs than ups, so many that I sometimes wonder if our life together is a constant downhill slope. But you know what they say, "Couples who suffer together, stay together." Or was it something else? Ah, never mind.

Now, Mita, she's got this insatiable wanderlust. She loves travelling more than I love a good nap, which, trust me, is a lot. I mean, who can blame her? Exploring new places, trying new foods, and collecting passport stamps—it's all very exciting, I'm sure. But here's the thing: I like to take things slow and easy when I travel. I'm the kind of person who enjoys a leisurely stroll through a picturesque village, while Mita's idea of fun is bungee jumping off the Eiffel Tower!

I've taken her to parts of Europe, Thailand, and Greece, and she's even ventured to the USA to stay with her Uncle for a whole month. But despite all that, her obsession with travel is unyielding. She dreams of cruising on a ship that's probably bigger than our house, embarking on the Trans-Siberian Express from Moscow to Vladivostok, or doing something so adventurous that I can't even fill in the blank.

Every day, like clockwork, she watches travel programs on TV. I'm convinced she's seen more of Europe, the USA, Australia, New Zealand and Latin American countries from the comfort of our couch than most people see in a lifetime. It's like she's on a virtual world tour while I'm here, mastering the art of channel surfing!

But, alas, we're not exactly rolling in dough these days. So, fulfilling Mita's grand travel dreams is a bit like trying to fill a swimming pool with a leaky bucket—pointless and wet. Yet, she continues to dream, and I can't help but admire her tenacity. Who am I to stand in the way of her dreams? After all, there's no harm in getting a little obsessed and dreaming big.

So, here's to Mita, the queen of wanderlust, the empress of adventure, and the champion of travel dreams. May her adventures always be epic, her itineraries forever packed, and her passport pages filled with stamps. Happy dreaming, Mita! Ha ha ha... and maybe, just maybe, one day, we'll find a way to make those dreams come true (or at least get you a nice travel-themed jigsaw puzzle to pass the time). ◇◈✈❤

- Udayan

25

From Teetotaler to Tippler: A Spirited Journey

Cheers to Curiosity, Compromises, and Love on the Rocks!
Ah, the saga of my dance with the devil's nectar! Back in my teenage years, alcohol was about as appealing as a porcupine's embrace. You see, my dear old Dad, a fine soldier, dabbled in the occasional tipple at those rowdy mess parties. A merry sight, I assure you.

Then came the fateful day when I reached the age of reckoning. Dad, in his infinite wisdom, extended the invite to join the revelry. At first, I conjured excuses like a magician in a hurry. But curiosity, that mischievous imp, got the better of me, and I found myself face-to-face with rum and cola. The taste? Let's just say it was like a bad date - memorable for all the wrong reasons.

Fast forward, and I found myself donning the hat of an engineer in the city of Hyderabad. Beer was my occasional companion, an old friend who popped in for a visit maybe thrice or four times a year. Then, destiny called again, and off I went to Gurgaon, where I met the boisterous Shyamalda, who had a penchant for proclaiming, "He who abstains from drink fears the wrath of his better half!" Oh, the gospel truth in those words.

And so, I graduated from sipping to socializing. Evenings, post office and relaxed Sundays turned into spirited discussions on matters of state and the world's affairs. Now, when it comes to imbuing spirits and dealing with spouses, well, let's just say I had my fair share of altercations post these revelries. My dear wife, Mita, harboured a vehement distaste for the liquid fire, fueled by the dramatic portrayals of Hindi cinema, where it transformed men into pillaging monsters. Those movies, she adored with a passion.

Desperate to bridge this alcoholic abyss, I hatched a cunning plan. A bottle of white wine became my peace envoy. After a series of refusals,

Mita succumbed to curiosity's wily charm. Slowly but surely, she tiptoed into the world of alcoholic elixirs.

Now, three decades later, I've bid adieu to the spirited pursuits, thanks to the unruly duo of diabetes and a difficult kidney. Alas! Mita yearns for those occasional tipples we once shared. But, in a twist of fate, she's been dealt the early stages of the same diabetic hand. She's sworn off the spirits, which, I suppose, is a silver lining, save for the fact that she pines for those delightful white and red wines. Oh, the irony!

- Udayan

26

Masterpieces in Stone: The Legacy of Priceless Craftmanship

Every Chisel Mark, Every Stroke of Paint, a Testament to Timeless Artistry

On a seemingly uneventful weekend, my husband, Udayan, and I embarked on an extraordinary expedition to the Ajanta and Ellora caves, nestled a considerable 250 kilometres away from our Pune abode. These caves, renowned for their intricate depictions of Hindu, Jain, and Buddhist ideologies, had long captivated our imaginations through the pages of history books. Now, the opportunity to witness the amalgamation of these three faiths in one sacred place was finally within our grasp.

The journey, though extensive, unfolded like a living tapestry, painting a serene tableau of nature's grandeur. With the car window down, a gentle breeze kissed my skin, and sporadic raindrops lent an air of tranquillity. We paused midday for a sumptuous meal, while the mellifluous tunes in the car seemed to lift our spirits.

Upon our arrival at the Ambassador Hotel, we were met with warm smiles, a gracious Namaste, and refreshing face towels. Our room beckoned with soft melodies playing in the background. After a brief exploration of the hotel's verdant grounds, we retired for the day, wearied by the journey's length.

The next morning, we set forth for the Ajanta Caves, a mere 65 kilometres away. The winding road and oncoming traffic made for a leisurely yet picturesque drive. Upon reaching the caves, we parked our car and boarded a bus that would ferry us higher into the hills. There, we enlisted the aid of a guide and a palanquin for Udayan, whose diabetic neuropathy hindered his ascent.

The sight that unfolded before us was nothing short of mesmerizing. The caves' meticulous carvings and the intricate frescoes inside bore testament to the incredible perseverance and artistry of their creators. Our guide regaled us with invaluable insights into the history of the Ajanta Caves.

These rock-hewn Buddhist cave sanctuaries and monasteries, nestled near Ajanta village in Maharashtra, stand as paragons of exquisite wall artistry. Carved into granite cliffs along a ravine, they bear witness to ancient Indian craftsmanship. Excavated between the 1st century BCE and the 7th century CE, these sanctuaries comprise worship halls and monastic dwellings. The true marvel, however, lies in the vivid frescoes depicting Buddhist legends and celestial beings.

After this awe-inspiring visit, we returned to our hotel, our hearts brimming with admiration for this extraordinary testament to human creativity. The subsequent day, we embarked on our journey to the Ellora Caves, located approximately 100 kilometres west of Ajanta. These caves, a synthesis of Buddhist, Hindu, and Jain influences, embody the spirit of tolerance that was characteristic of ancient India. The monuments are epic examples of Unity in Diversity amongst people of different faiths in the country.

As we made our way back to the hotel, my thoughts turned to our nation's potential, akin to a splendid garden of blossoms. It struck me that if only our politicians could emancipate themselves from their confines, India could indeed flourish and stand united. I couldn't help but ponder how long it might take for them to realize this vision and restore India to its golden era.

-Metali

27

The Luminescent Comedy: Navigating Marriage with the Left Hand Syndrome

When Conservation Meets Nonconformity, Love Shines Through the Darkness!

Ah, the Left Hand Syndrome! It sounds like a peculiar superpower only possessed by the chosen few. Mita, my wife, must be on a mission to save the world, one light switch at a time, with the power of her trusty left hand. It's like she's conducting a clandestine operation to put those annoying photons back in their place!

I am on the other side of this luminescent battle. I've valiantly tried to reason with Mita, explaining the intricacies of electricity consumption, and comparing it to geysers, ovens, fridges, and air conditioners that consume more electricity than lights. But alas, my pleas seem to ricochet off her like tiny bolts of electricity, leaving me in a state of resigned enlightenment.

She's got a point, though. We all do yap on about sustainability, don't we? In a world where we're tossing around words like "carbon footprint" and "ecological balance," perhaps Mita is the unsung hero, the champion of the kilowatts, fighting for the greater good, one switch at a time.

Yet, here I am, living in a house that sometimes resembles a cellar. It's daytime, but the clouds have conspired to turn my abode into a gloomy cavern. Mita, the eco-vigilante, stands tall, unyielding. "Switch on only when it is required," she declares as if the shadows themselves answer to her command.

So, I've raised the white flag, surrendering to a life in partial darkness. I've learned to navigate my own home like a ninja, relying on my other senses to guide me. Who needs sight when one has the keen instincts of a nocturnal creature, right?

In the grand tapestry of life, Mita's Left Hand Syndrome has woven a unique thread. It's a tale of peculiar conservation, a comedy of lights, and a lesson in finding a balance between sustainable living and keeping the lights on. Who knew marriage could be so illuminating?

- Udayan

28

Illuminating Hearts: A Journey of Education and Unity

Spreading the Light of Learning, One Person at a Time

My husband was nearing completion of his first book which I had co-authored with him. The satisfaction was immense, particularly given the challenging year he'd endured, marked by numerous hospitalizations. In those reflective moments, I would read to him from a diverse array of texts—Buddhist, Hindu, and the uplifting works of Dr. Daisaku Ikeda. It was during these times that he resolved to embark on his own writing journey, a decision that filled me with joy. Within a month, he had established his own blog, not only chronicling his personal experiences but also committing to penning a book about his father. Our family had weathered significant hardships after the loss of our business, fighting tooth and nail to keep the hearth fires burning and ensuring our children received an education amidst adversity. My elder son took on employment and managed MBA classes, often attending them two or three times a week, with understanding teachers granting him attendance for the remainder. Looking back now, I am filled with gratitude that my father-in-law imparted the values that have enabled us to guide our children toward successful lives, emphasizing unity.

Sending the book for publication with Udayan was a source of immense satisfaction. He had laboured tirelessly, producing the book in a record time of just over two months, incorporating my own contributions. As a follower of Buddhism, I felt compelled to conduct several home visits, dedicated to furthering the teachings of Dr. Daisaku Ikeda. I firmly believe that imparting even a single line of wisdom to a member not only bestows good fortune but also elevates one's own life condition, allowing the pursuit of human revolution day by day, year after year. A scheduling mishap left me without a prior appointment with a member, but my mentor's advice echoed in my mind: to pray and persist in my mission, undeterred by any obstacles.

With prayers in my heart and my mentor's blessings, I embarked on a cab journey to the member's residence. Upon arrival, a profound silence hung over the house, leaving me momentarily taken aback. Puzzled, I deliberated on my next move. Should I leave or inquire about the cause of this unusual hush? After some heartfelt prayers, clarity emerged: I had a purpose, and I must meet her. Summoning my courage, I entered the house, only to be met with the news that the member's mother-in-law had passed away. Back at home, I offered fervent prayers for this woman who had been a steadfast supporter. While she was alive, I had bestowed upon her a copy of my book, Bouquet of Poems, an assortment of poems on World Peace and youth, seeking her blessings by touching her feet. Her endorsement of my work had been a source of great comfort, encouraging me to forge ahead with my mission of illuminating minds through education. Her words echoed in my ears, and tears flowed freely down my cheeks. She was another pillar of support, alongside my mother, in my mission to kindle the flame of learning in those whose hearts were dimmed and resources limited.

It is through the light of education that the entire cosmos is illuminated within an individual. Let us adopt the principle of "each one teach one." This is the pressing need of our time and civilization. After my prayers, I resolved to press on with my mission to educate all who yearned to learn. If it is the will of the divine, I will endeavour to establish a primary education centre, open to all.

-Metali

29

Ganesha's Grand Gala

Celebrating Ganesha with Gusto, but Let's Keep the Volume in Check!

[illegible]

Vakratunda Mahakaya

Surya Koti Sama Prabha

Nirvighnam Kuru Me Deva

Sarva Karyesu Sarvada.

"Vakratunda Mahakaya, Surya Koti Sama Prabha," or as I like to call it, the elephant-sized tongue-twister of divine invocation! You see, in the colourful realm of Hindu mythology, there's a God who goes by the name Ganesha. He's the big guy with an elephant head, and he's the go-to deity when you're about to kickstart something big, like a new project or maybe just your day.

Now, Ganesha isn't your typical deity. He's got a potbelly that would make Santa Claus jealous, and he's got this thing for Indian sweets. Seriously, the guy loves his desserts. But what really sets him apart is his ride – a bandicoot rat. Yes, you heard me right, a rat! It's like Ganesha is saying, "I can overcome any obstacle, even if it's as small as a rat or as big as an elephant."

So, people in India love celebrating Ganesha during the Ganesh festival, especially in Maharashtra. It's a 10-day extravaganza, and you can't miss it even if you tried. But here's the catch – it's not all sweet and serene. The celebrations can get so wild that the police are left scratching their heads. I'm talking laser shows, blaring music that can wake up the dead, and speakers that could shake the earth.

Now, don't get me wrong; I love a good party as much as the next person. But when the decibel levels are breaking the sound barrier, it's a different story. It's not just about annoying those from other faiths;

it's about making life miserable for the sick and elderly. I mean, come on, do we really need to celebrate so loudly that even Ganesha himself would need some earplugs?

Festivals are our way of expressing our beliefs and having a blast, but they should come with a side of social responsibility. Let's keep the celebrations within the limits of decency, folks. After all, even the God of Beginnings wouldn't want to begin his day with a massive headache!

-Udayan

30

Embracing Hinduism: A Personal Journey of Faith and Philosophy

Navigating the Depths of Belief, Ritual, and Philosophy in Hinduism, Guided by a Father's Wisdom

I hold a firm belief in the existence of a higher power, which some may refer to as God. However, I do not engage in the customary practices of temples or the sacred rituals performed at home, such as puja and yagna, which are integral to the Hindu faith. Speaking of Hinduism, I identify myself as a Hindu by faith, even though I do not adhere to its customary rites. In my opinion, every individual has the autonomy to follow their own beliefs, whether it be Hinduism, Christianity, Buddhism, Sikhism, or any other.

Regrettably, I haven't had the opportunity to deeply explore the tenets of Hinduism due to my perpetual pursuit of providing for my family. Nevertheless, I gleaned certain customs from my father, whom I closely emulated in life. My affection for my parents is genuine, and it is not solely because I am articulating this; it is a sentiment that I truly hold. Throughout my life, particularly in emulating my father, I've come to revere him. From my early years, he instilled in me the perspective that Hinduism transcends religion; it is a way of life, a philosophical outlook. He elucidated this distinction by teaching me about Dharma and Panth. While Hinduism or Sanatan is the Dharma for humanity, its panths encompass Sikhism, Islam, Christianity, and others, which emerged less than two and a half millennia ago. Sanatan Dharma, on the other hand, predates even ten thousand years, as attested by the ancient Vedic scriptures and the epics of Ramayana and Mahabharata. Ramayana was written roughly five centuries before the birth of Christ, and Mahabharata about three decades before his advent. Dharma embodies timeless values, while panth or sect pertains to specific beliefs, distinct forms of deity worship, and the like.

Hinduism or Sanatan Dharma has been in existence for approximately six thousand years and is also referred to as the Vedic religion.

I wholeheartedly embrace the theory imparted to me by my father and take pride in being a devout Hindu, despite not being a regular temple-goer. I did, however, initiate and partake in the annual Durga Puja celebrations. I've organized this event on both small and grand scales, with preparations commencing at least two months in advance. We would collectively rehearse for songs, dances, and theatrical performances scheduled for all five days of festivity – Sashthi, Saptomi, Ashtami, Navami, and Dashami. These days were dedicated to the worship of the Goddess Durga, with purohits offering prayers to the imposing idol(s) as described below. This celebration commemorates Durga's triumph over Mahishasura and is observed fervently by the global Hindu community. According to Hindu scriptures, this festival signifies the victory of goddess Durga in her battle against Mahishasura, the embodiment of evil. Therefore, it epitomizes the conquest of righteousness over malevolence. Alongside the image of Ma Durga, there are smaller depictions of Ganesh, Kartikey, Lakshmi, and Saraswati. They symbolize Wisdom and Understanding, Courageousness, Vigor, Wealth, and Knowledge and Art, respectively. These deities are the two sons and two daughters of Durga.

Apart from Durga Puja, I scarcely recall commemorating any festival with such exuberance, except for the modest observance of Diwali, the festival of lights. I ardently adhere to the principle that "work is wisdom," and this has been the guiding ethos of my life. I have both upheld and tried to disseminate this philosophy to every member of my family.

- Udayan

31

The Ten Worlds in Buddhist Practice: A Journey of Self-Discovery

Explore the Ten Worlds: Your Path to Inner Wisdom and Enlightenment

Envision a typical Monday morning scene: The blaring alarm disrupts your deep slumber, prompting a reluctant groan as you coax yourself out of bed to draw back the curtains, revealing a rainy day. After getting dressed, you head to the kitchen, where you set the kettle on, tend to your dog, and settle down for breakfast. As you peruse the cereal box, you're intrigued to find that your bowl of cornflakes provides a significant portion of the recommended daily intake of various essential vitamins. Just then, the flap of the letterbox jingles, revealing two envelopes – one from the electricity board and the other from the income tax office. Fearing the worst, you opt to open the electricity bill first, only to be met with shock at its exorbitant amount. You resolve to compose a stern letter to the electricity board as soon as you get to work, convinced they must have made a mistake. However, a nagging thought crosses your mind – it was an exceptionally cold winter, and you did leave the heating on through most of the night. Your spirits sink; they might be right after all. If so, it could mean sacrificing your summer vacation plans. With a heavy heart, you gingerly open the foreboding brown envelope from the Inland Revenue, only to find a tax rebate! It more than covers the electricity bill, leaving you with plenty to spare for your holiday. You can't help but let out a triumphant cheer before heading off to work, blissfully oblivious to the pouring rain...

In this seemingly ordinary morning scenario, you've traversed nine of the Ten Worlds, a pivotal concept in Buddhism. These Ten Worlds encapsulate ten fundamental inner states of being that we all cycle through, moment by moment. To briefly elaborate, they encompass

- Hell (suffering),

- Hunger (desire-driven state),
- Animality (instinctive behaviour),
- Anger (competitive or conflicted state),
- Tranquillity (a state of peace and calm),
- Rapture (temporary joy from desire fulfilment),
- Learning (acquiring knowledge from external teachings),
- Realization (personal understanding through self-effort),
- Bodhisattva (self-sacrifice and joy through aiding others), and
- Buddhahood (absolute happiness attained through Bodhisattva actions).

These states, ranging from suffering to ultimate happiness, form the core of the human experience, influenced by both external factors and inner endeavours. Let us analyze our daily life as enumerated above.

Firstly, while asleep, you are in the state of Tranquillity. Sleep does not automatically mean Tranquillity. If you were having a nightmare, for instance, you would be in the state of Hell, and if you were dreaming of your lover you might well be in the state of Rapture – or not, as the case may be. Then the alarm goes. You wake up because the state of Animality is momentarily activated: in this case, manifesting itself as the instinct of fear. As soon as you are awake and realize you are not being attacked, the knowledge that you have to get out of your warm and comfortable bed to face once more the rigours of the world plunges you, even though only momentarily, straight into Hell. Seeing that it is raining keeps you there. As you get dressed, however, Animality reasserts itself as you start to feel hungry. You might logically think that feeling hungry means you are in a state of Hunger but, as Daisaku Ikeda further explains, 'There is a difference between the hunger whose source is voraciousness and the hunger that comes from normal instinct, and this is the difference between those in the state of Hunger and those in the mindless state of Animality'. Driven by Animality into the kitchen, you start to prepare breakfast. Once again, though, your state changes when the dog growls and you realize, after a moment's thought, that she is probably feeling hungry too. That realization, indeed all the realizations you have had since waking up, are very minor instances of the world of Realization in your life. Deciding to feed the dog is an example of Bodhisattva nature at work; while reading the back of the cornflakes packet finds you in the state of Learning. Then the letters arrive. Fear at the sight of letters that could contain bad news is another example of Animality, and your assumption that the electricity bill is wrong is an example of the state of Anger. It is important to note that one does not necessarily have to be angry to be in a state of Anger. Anger here is characterized by a contentious and arrogant attitude toward others – 'those stupid bureaucrats' at the electricity board, in this instance. It does not matter that the bill might very well be wrong: Anger shows itself in your automatic reaction that you are in the right. A moment later, as you think back to the winter, Anger passes away and Hell reappears. Your dream of a summer holiday, a true manifestation of the state of Hunger, the world of desires, seems impossible. And then, as you discover you have got a generous tax rebate, the world of Rapture explodes into your life. In fact, so strong is it that it completely changes your attitude towards the day. The things that before were prompting the state of Hell to manifest itself, like the weather and the thought of going to work, now appear to be not so bad after all. But they have not changed –you have, at least a dozen times since waking up. This is a gross underestimation of our real changeability; it is theoretically possible to analyse in even more minute detail the myriad changes we experience within ourselves from moment to moment.

Buddhism, a philosophy and spiritual tradition that originated over two millennia ago in ancient India, offers profound insights into the nature of existence and the human psyche. Central to Buddhist teachings is the concept of the Ten Worlds, which presents a comprehensive framework for understanding the various states of human existence, ranging from suffering to enlightenment. This essay delves into the essence of the Ten Worlds, exploring each realm and its implications for personal growth and spiritual development.

The Ten Worlds, often depicted in a circular diagram known as the Wheel of Life, represent ten distinct psychological states or realms that individuals can experience. These realms encompass both positive and negative aspects of human consciousness, providing a holistic view of the human condition. Each world is characterized by a dominant state of mind, which influences one's perceptions, actions, and experiences.

-(Abridged from The Buddha in Daily Life by Richard Causton)

About the Author

Udayan and Metali, who have been devoted to each other for a remarkable span of forty-two years, with a three-year courtship that preceded their union, reside in a tranquil enclave of Pune, where they've carved out their own private world. Metali, a seasoned educator with two decades of experience, recently unveiled her poetic masterpiece, "Bouquet of Poems." Her unwavering commitment to the principles of Buddhism is evident in her daily routine, which is often filled with prayers for global harmony, gatherings with fellow practitioners, and the noble pursuit of inspiring others to embrace the path of peaceful coexistence.

Udayan, on the other hand, embarked on a fulfilling engineering career that spanned several years in the automotive manufacturing sector. Notably, he also dedicated a portion of his professional journey to imparting knowledge as a lecturer in Strategic Operations Management and Supply Chain Management. A prolific author in his own right, Udayan has already gifted the literary world with his work, "Jagat Bandhu," and is on the brink of introducing two more books to his readers.

Their legacy extends beyond the realm of literature, as they are blessed with two sons. One has attained proficiency in finance management, while the other has carved out a successful career in information technology. Their elder son has also graced them with a delightful grandson, who is around eleven years old, bringing boundless joy to their lives.

Even in their well-deserved retirement, this couple continues to wield the pen, crafting books and snippets whenever inspiration strikes, for it is their chosen means of enriching their retired lives with creativity and purpose.